EXTREME PETS!

Author: Jane Harrington
Designer: Bill Henderson

Copyright © 2006 Scholastic Inc.

Tangerine
Press

an imprint of
SCHOLASTIC
www.scholastic.com

Scholastic and Tangerine Press and associated logos are trademarks of Scholastic Inc.

Published by Tangerine Press, an imprint of Scholastic Inc., 557 Broadway, New York, NY 10012

10 9 8 7 6 5 4 3 2

ISBN 0-439-82948-8
Printed and bound in China

Dear X-Pet Fans,

Did you know that there are actually OVER 130 MILLION cats and dogs in the United States? This may raise a troubling question in your mind, like: WHAT if they got ORGANIZED? They could take their feline and canine freedoms on the march, STORM Washington, and the next thing you know, we'd all be lapping our food out of large bowls and drooling on each other's sneakers. Doesn't this WORRY YOU??

Yeah, me neither. But aren't you just a teeny bit bored waiting for your beloved furball to do something EXCITING? Of COURSE you are. That's why you're HERE. You SHUN the ordinary! You LONG for something TOTALLY different! I mean, can a dog grow a new leg if he happens to lose one? Does wearing your cat around your neck make people shoot right off the sidewalk as you pass them? NO! Can EXTREME PETS do these things? OH yeah.

So the REAL question is: WHICH X-PET IS RIGHT FOR YOU? And THAT is what this handbook is ALL ABOUT. On these pages you will find IMPORTANT INFORMATION about a whole bunch of SWEET pets, like...HEDGEHOGS! SNAKES! CHINCHILLAS! ENORMOUS COCKROACHES! And by the time you're done reading, you will KNOW your PERFECT PET—the one that is REALLY FUN; the one that your parents will NEVER, in a million years, let you HAVE.

But don't despair! The last section of this handbook is ALL ABOUT ensnaring—OOPS, I mean PREPARING—your parents for the very delicate question you must ask them. Just follow the easy step-by-step guide, and results are GUARANTEED! (What those results ARE is another matter, but one has to have HOPE.)

The Pet Whiz

P.S. To make sure you are picking a pet that YOU can care for, and one that is RIGHT FOR YOUR FAMILY, complete THE EXTREME PET PACT on the next page. Your family will thank you, and your pet will thank you. (But not in words. Hopefully.)

The Extreme Pet Pact

Before getting an extreme pet, I, _____, vow to do all of the following things:

___ Learn as much as I can about the pet so I know if it's right for me and my family.

___ Teach my parents/guardians about it, and make sure they are able to help with care.

___ Find out if anyone in my family is allergic or has an illness that could make them sick with this pet around.

___ If there are babies or younger kids at home, make sure there is a way to keep the pet away from them so they will not get bitten or harmed in any way.

___ Plan for where the pet will live and how much it will cost to get and keep it.

___ Create a schedule or chart to help me remember to feed and clean up after the pet.

___ Make sure there is someone who can pet-sit when I am on vacation.

___ Figure out if the pet will need any shots, check-ups, or other medical care, and if so, find the nearest veterinarian who can do it.

___ Remember that my pet is a living thing that needs me.

Signed,

_____

CORN SNAKE

SO COOL IT'S COLD... BLOODED!

THIS is the ULTIMATE pet if you have been yearning to freak out members of your family or get rid of those pesky visitors to your home.* Corn snakes are pretty mellow, and they like being held. Human warm-bloodedness feels good to them since their cold-blooded bodies can't make any heat of its own. You can easily hold it in your hands, or (FASHION STATEMENT!) put it around your neck like a scarf.

*Works best if the snake is kept in a central location in the house, such as the living room.

THE SUITABLE SNAKE SPACE

In the wild, corn snakes live in forests and other natural places, and they spend most of their free time hanging out underground in rodent burrows. Since you (hopefully) don't have any of those in your home, you can keep a corn snake in a glass aquarium tank—a 20-gallon (76-liter) tank will work for the life of your snake. Snakes aren't known to be fussy about interior decorating, so you don't need anything fancy in there. Substrate (that's pet jargon for stuff to put on the bottom) can be purchased at any pet store —the

biodegradable, paper-based bedding is probably best for the planet. You'll also need a decent-sized, heavy water dish and something for the snake to hide in, since it spends a lot of time doing that. An empty cereal box works well for this, and you can change it periodically for variety — Cheerios® one week, Fruity Pebbles® the next — depending on your mood (or the snake's).

REAL IMPORTANT: The tank will need a secure screen top, or else your snake will soon escape and live under the floorboards of your house, causing family members to lunge into walls at the slightest sound of rustling. (While this might be somewhat amusing, it will soon grow old, and you'll wish you had your snake for company, since no one in your house will be speaking to you.)

THE SATISFYING SNAKE SNACK

If you observe a corn snake eating in its natural environment, you would first see it biting its prey (a rodent or bat, for instance), then constricting it by violently slapping its coils around it and tightening until the critter expired from suffocation.

Report Card

HOW does this pet RANK?

Coolness	A
Aroma	A
(If you happen to leave an old, uneaten mouse in there for two weeks.)	F
Neatness	B
Ease of Care	B
Cost Factor	C

SCI-NAME: *Elaphe guttata*, or "spotted deer."

SIZE: 2 ½–5 ft. (.8–1.5 m) Record length is 6 ft. (1.8 m)

LIFESPAN: About 10 to 15 years. Record is 23 years in captivity.

After that you would see the snake unhinge its jaw by opening its mouth very wide, and then you would see it swallow the prey whole, even though the prey might be ten times bigger than the snake's head. If you were still observing at this point — and not running through the woods, retching — you would then see a lump move down the long body of the snake, getting smaller and smaller as the reptile's digestive juices broke down the animal's bodily organs and bones, until the only thing left to be expelled later from the snake's other end (technically: the vent) would be a little pile of fur. For those of you who are thinking, "Whoa—that is COOL!" the bad news is that you probably won't be able to witness this entire feeding frenzy sequence at home. This is because it is best to feed already-dead mice to captive snakes. And anyway, your snake will be smart enough to recognize when something is already dead and won't bother with all the constricting and slapping and suffocating. The rest of the eating routine is pretty much the same, though, and you can have many years of enjoying the show through the glass walls of your snake's tank. (Or not, if you prefer.) Besides feeding, the only other things you need to do to keep your snake healthy are: Keep the tank clean, and make sure there is always a full dish of fresh water (because they need to drink it, and sometimes like to take a soak before they shed their skin).

ASK THE PET WHIZ

Q: Why shouldn't I feed live mice to pet snakes?

A: Mice can attack snakes. And I don't mean evil, R. L. Stine mice, but ANY mice. You see, sometimes snakes just don't WANT to eat. This can be because they are getting ready to shed, or it can be because they just aren't hungry. A mouse that is suddenly dropped into a tank with a snake doesn't know this, however, and it becomes very scared. Scared animals tend to bite, and since the snake is trapped in the tank with the mouse, it tends to get bitten. This isn't good for your snake, you would have to agree. But don't be disappointed —it's actually pretty fun having dead mice around the house.

Q: Uh, how is it FUN having dead mice around the house?

A: I'm glad you asked! First of all, the places you buy dead mice have a sense of humor. And when the mice arrive in the mail, they are all lined up in a big zip-lock bag, which you can put in your freezer. (WARNING: THEY WILL BE PACKED IN DRY ICE, WHICH CAN BE REALLY DANGEROUS, SO GET AN ADULT TO UNPACK THE BOX!!) Consider the hours of joy you will get from hearing the screams of your teenage sister's friends when they're rooting around for some ice cream on movie night at your house…or seeing the expression on Grandpa's face when he puts his glasses on to realize those were not chicken legs he was getting ready to deep fry for dinner. It's mind-boggling how much entertainment can come from a bag of frozen mice!

Q: So, snakes eat the mice frozen?

A: Uh, no. You have to defrost them. The best method is to take one or two mice out of the freezer (depending on how much your snake eats at one time) and seal the frozen mice in a plastic bag, then drop this into a cup of warm water and leave it there until it's thawed. (For extra kicks, pretend you are making a cup of mouse tea.) NEVER thaw a mouse in the microwave oven. If you do this, you may never get the smell of cooked mouse out of it, and you'll have to throw the oven away, and maybe even move out of your house.

Continued on page 10

9

ASK THE PET WHIZ

Q: I forget to do things every day — like brushing my teeth and doing my homework. Do you think I can take care of a corn snake?
A: This, my friend, is the PERFECT pet for you, because they only eat about once a week. Most reptiles can even go for months without eating.

Q: Is it gross cleaning up snake poop?
A: Since snakes only eat once a week, they only defecate (technical term for poop) about once a week. You can scoop the dirty substrate out with a plastic bag, like you would if you were walking a dog (only you don't have to then walk around your neighborhood carrying the bag of poop, so it's a whole lot less embarrassing). (Raise your hand if you've run into a friend or a cute girl/boy while carrying a bag of dog poop.)

Q: How come corn snakes can digest BONES, which are very hard, but not FUR, which is very soft?
A: It has something to do with enzymes. Or maybe they just don't like fur. Which means if you were a really NICE snake owner, you would de-fur all food before giving it to the snake — you know, like when your mom took the crusts off your sandwiches when you were little.

Q: Does it feel creepy to have a snake slithering around on you?
A: Well, actually, NO! This is an AWESOME pet to hold. Snakeskin is very smooth and dry, and not slimy, as the anti-snake people of the world would have you believe. It is, in fact, very soothing to have a snake curling around your hands and arms, and through your hair. It's like meditation. Yoga programs would probably be a whole lot more effective if they added snakes to their class activities.

Q: Do they have a poisonous bite?
A: This is probably not a question YOU would ask, since WHO

WOULD WANT A POISONOUS SNAKE, but this is NO DOUBT a question you will be asked if you ever ask your parents if you can have a snake. So, NO, corn snakes are not poisonous. They do have teeth, and if they are hurt or very confused (say, you bathe your thumb in eau de mouse, and dangle it very mouse-like in front of them), then they could bite. (Sorry to ruin all your fun). But so can cats, and their teeth are sharper.

Q: Speaking of cats, can they live with snakes?
A: Definitely not in the same tank. Seriously, though, cats will spend an enormous amount of time trying to get into the snake tank, and when they're NOT doing that they'll be sleeping on top of it. So, if you have a cat, you need an extra-strong screen top, with an extra-good lock. (And if you have a cat that likes to bring you gifts of dead mice, then you will save some money on food for the snake.)

Q: If corn snakes live to be 10 or 15, or 23 years old, what do I do with it when I go to college?
A: You are thinking too much like an adult now, so I suggest IT'S TIME FOR YOU TO STOP THINKING. If your parent asks this question, though, I suggest you mumble the answer.

Q: Why are they called corn snakes?
A: Well, some people think it is the belly scales, because they look like maize, also known as Indian corn. Other people say the European settlers found them in corncribs or in cornfields, and they thought they were eating corn, though they would, of course, have been eating the mice or other furry things that were eating the corn. I'm sure the American Indians were having a good laugh about all this, and it makes a person wonder what THEY called these snakes.

Continued on page 13

SO, WHERE DO YOU GET CORN SNAKES?

The healthiest corn snakes will come from breeders, who go to reptile shows all over the country. You can go to one of these and pick out your own baby corn snake. The cost is usually about $40. If you can't find a reptile show or a breeder, you can check with your local pet store. They usually carry corn snakes, but it may vary from state to state.

BE A CORN SNAKE EXPERT

There are many cool things to know about corn snakes, and you should learn more before you decide this is the extreme pet for you. Talking to exotic pet vets or herpetologists (reptile gurus) at your local zoo is a good way to get going on this.

Strange factoids...

Snakes don't taste with their tongues –they SMELL with their tongues.

Corn snakes have only one lung.

Corn snakes never blink.

Corn snakes have a single row of belly scales, each corresponding to a single vertebra. (So you can tell how many vertebrae a snake has just by looking at its belly.)

Corn snakes are deaf. They have no ears at all.

Snakes shed their skin as they grow. They can crawl out of it all in one piece, and it comes off inside-out –sort of like a wet sock. COOL THING TO DO: Save these skins and hang them in your room to keep track of how much your snake has grown.

ASK THE PET WHIZ

Q: How do they get around, anyway, with no arms or legs?

A: Corn snakes have long, flat scales on their bellies cleverly referred to by snake scientists as "belly scales." A snake hitches these scales onto whatever surface it is on, and pulls itself along. If you put a snake on a piece of glass, it will freak out, and start flailing about, because it has nothing to hitch itself to. I know you are thinking, "Whoa! That sounds really COOL!" but it isn't nice to do this to your snake just so YOU can have a few laughs. Really.

Q: Isn't it kind of gross that they shed their skin?

A: No. Unless you think it's gross that humans shed their skin, because we DO. It just comes off in really teeny pieces, which is what a lot of the dust in your house is—

your family's skin. It would be a whole lot more fun if we shed it all in one piece, like snakes. Couldn't you picture the halls in school littered with the skins of humans? But I digress. Anyway, it's not, like, ALL the skin—just the top layer, which is all old and worn.

Q: My mom hates snakes.

A: That is not a question.

Q: OK. How do I get my mom to stop hating snakes?

A: Tell her the GOOD things about snakes. They are free exterminators, for instance. The world would be OVERRUN with rats and mice if it weren't for them, and before we could blink an eye, they'd have voting rights and be supporting candidates for Congress.

LEOPARD GECKO

THIS reptile is a favorite with teachers, but don't let that worry you! Leopard geckos are really interesting, and they need very little care and attention. Though they have bumpy skin, their soft scales and gentle nature make them easy to handle, and it's très cool to have one crawling up your arm with that side-to-side gecko swagger! THIS is an AWESOME pet.

GECKO CARE (SIMPLE FOR EVEN THE LAZIEST OF PET OWNERS!)

A gecko can live its whole life in a 10-gallon (38-liter) glass tank with a screen top. You can use newspaper or paper-based substrate on the bottom. A hide box (or two) can be made from a large margarine tub—just cut a doorway and turn it upside down in the tank. You'll also need a shallow, heavy water dish, and a rough stone or piece of bark to help with shedding.

Since these are desert-types, they do need a little extra warmth. An under-tank heater on one side of the tank is best. A light (any kind that gives heat) is also recommended, set on a timer so there are about 12 hours of light and dark each day. With a cheap thermometer strip on the wall of the tank, you can see if the temperature is right throughout the day. Ideal is 84–88°F (29–31°C) during the day, 70°F (21°C) at night.)

They need to eat a few mealworms or crickets each day. To keep your gecko healthy, you need to coat the bugs in vitamin/mineral powder—a fun activity! You put some powder in a little bag, add a few crickets or

Report Card

This gecko's honor roll (and on a roll!)

Coolness	A
Aroma	A
Neatness	A
Ease of Care	A
Cost Factor	B

SCI-NAME: *Eublepharis macularius*

SIZE: 6–9 in. (15–23 cm)

LIFESPAN: Up to 20 years!

mealworms, and SHAKE! (Gently — geckos won't eat dead bugs.) Put fresh water in the tank every day.

Cleanup is COMPLETELY painless. They defecate (uh, poop) in only one corner. You just scoop it out each day or so, and you're good to go!

Leopard geckos can be handled for up to about 20 minutes a day. They have claws (unlike most geckos, which have sticky toe-pads), but these are not sharp and never need to be trimmed. They hardly ever bite, and you can barely feel it when they do.

Various fun facts about leopard geckos….

SIT, BOY!

Yes, you can make your gecko sit! Put your hand over its back and gently curl your fingers under the gecko's stomach. It will sit on your hand.

AND WAG YOUR TAIL?

After geckos spot their food, they will sometimes wag their tails before darting to get it. COOL to watch!

BUILT-IN WINDSHIELD WIPERS

Leopard geckos clean their eyeballs with their tongues.

WOW! THIS ANIMAL DOESN'T PEE!

That's right, folks! It gets rid of waste (uric acid) in solid crystal form.

HOW IS A LEOPARD GECKO LIKE A CAMEL?

These two animals may not look at all alike, but they have a lot in common. They both come from desert climates, and they both store large amounts of fat in their bodies. Camels store it in their humps, and leopard geckos store in their tails. They can use the fat to keep them nourished when food and water is scarce. (And, yes, this means your gecko will be okay if you forget to feed it now and then.)

Q: Someone told me that leopard geckos can lose their tails. Is this true?

A: Yes. When a leopard gecko is caught by the tail (by a predator or very clumsy human), it can make a quick getaway by snapping its tail off between spaces in the tailbone. Just IMAGINE the possibilities if we could do this with OUR body parts! One minute your teacher would have you by the elbow, marching you to the principal's office, and the next minute she'd be standing there in the hall, shrieking, a detached arm in her hand! Wouldn't that be GREAT?

Q: Well, only if you could grow it back.

A: Exactly the point! And leopard geckos CAN grow their tails back. It takes a while, though, and they are kind of prone to illness while that's happening. So you should really do your best to keep your gecko in one piece at all times.

Q: How do I tell if my gecko is male or female?

A: If it's over one month old, you can tell by looking at the base of the tail, behind the back legs. If it's a male, there will be a row of V-shaped pores. If not, then it's a female (duh).

Continued on page 19

GIMME SOME SKIN...
TO EAT?!

Leopard geckos eat their skin as they shed it. Some people find this disgusting, but this is the way geckos get calcium. And since they don't have little refrigerators stocked with milk and ice cream, they're sort of stuck with this method. (Gecko skin is really interesting, so try to get a look at it before it's eaten—you can see the little toes and stuff.)

ASK THE PET WHIZ

Q: I have a bunch of crickets jumping around in my basement, and I want to catch them for my gecko. Is that okay?

A: You sure know how to have fun! Seriously, though, the answer to your question is: maybe. If your house has had any pesticide treatments (for cockroaches, termites, etc.), then the crickets could be contaminated, and you don't want to feed them to your gecko.

Q: My gecko has a hole in his head. Is this normal?

A: For a leopard gecko, yes. When you look in the ear hole, you can see clear through and out the other side. VERY freaky.

BLUE-TONGUED SKINK

NO, this reptile didn't get into your stash of blue-razz lollipops! These lizards have cobalt-blue tongues they waggle around in their bright pink mouths to scare away predators. Blue-tongued skinks are good pets because they're completely calm and cool (but kind of costly), and they move at a snail's pace. Literally. (That's what they eat in the wild.)

AT HOME WITH YOUR SKINK

In their natural range, blue-tongues are often kept outside in gardens, but you will probably have to keep yours in a cage or tank. Since an adult skink can be as long as a loaf of Italian bread, you'll need something that's about four feet long (1.2 m). A 40- to 55-gallon (151- to 208-liter) tank with a screen top will make your skink very happy.

Blue-tongued skinks have legs that are seriously short and small, so you definitely don't need anything in the tank for climbing. It will want places to hide, though, and this can be accomplished with cardboard boxes and newspapers.

Since blue-tongues are from a hot part of the planet, you'll need to warm the tank with lights and an under-tank heater. A basking area will need to stay at about 95°F (35°C) all day, and the rest of the tank should be in the 75° to 85°F (24° to 29°C) range. At night, temperatures can drop about 10°. Skinks require some humidity, so you'll need to spray the tank with a fine mist of water every couple of days.

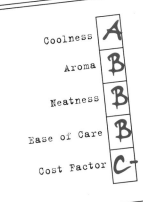

Report Card

Coolness	A
Aroma	B
Neatness	B
Ease of Care	B
Cost Factor	C-

LITTLE FACTOIDS...

Blue-tongued skinks have moveable,
transparent lower eyelids to keep out
dust and dirt.

SCI-NAME: *Tiliqua*
Australian species: *scincoides intermedia*
or *scincoides scincoides*
New Guinea and Indonesian species: *gigas*

SIZE: 17–24 in. (43–61 cm)

LIFESPAN: 10 to 20 years

ASK THE WHIZ

Like snakes, skinks smell with their tongues. The tongues bring air particles to the Jacobsen's organ at the back of the mouth, where smells are processed.

Natural predators include the Tasmanian devil, dingoes, and kookaburras.

Q: My baby skink is always hissing at me. What should I do? I'm getting an inferiority complex.
A: There is probably nothing wrong with your skink. They're usually feisty when young, but they relax a whole lot as they get older. If it keeps up, though, you could try a psychologist (to help you with that inferiority complex).

Q: Help! My skink is eating rocks! What do I do?
A: Uh, nothing. Skinks sometimes eat little rocks to help them digest their food. (Birds do this, too.) So make sure you keep a little pile of small stones in the tank.

VEILED
CHAMELEON

YOU may consider tossing out your TV if you get one of these, because they're THAT COOL to watch. This large, leaf-shaped reptile can transform into an array of cartoon colors and patterns, swivel its eyeballs in different directions at the same time, and suck up its prey with a projectile tongue that's longer than its own body. There's no perfect pet, though—this one can bite, and it's pretty high maintenance.

THE CHALLENGES OF CHAMELEON CARE

While it may not cost a whole lot to buy and house a young veiled chameleon, they quickly grow up and demand a lot of space. An adult needs a cage that's about 3 feet (.9m) wide, 3 feet deep, and 4 feet (1.2m) high. Because ventilation is important, the sides should ideally be made of screening. (You will save a ton of money on the enclosure if you can find someone to help you make one.)

Since veiled chameleons are arboreal (live in trees), you have to put lots of leafy branches in the cage for climbing and hiding. There should be a basking area at the top, with a heat lamp on during the day. The basking spot should be around 100°F (38°C), and the rest of the cage should be in the 80sF

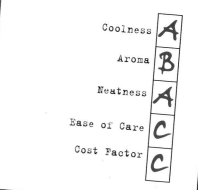

Report Card

Coolness **A**

Aroma **B**

Neatness **A**

Ease of Care **C**

Cost Factor **C**

SCI-NAME: *Chamaeleo calyptratus*
SIZE (from head to tip of tail): Females, 10–14 in. (25–36 cm); Males, 17–24 in. (43–61 cm)
LIFESPAN: Approximately 5 years for females, 8 years for males.

(30sC) during the day, and 60sF to 70sF (16°C to 21°C) at night. This may require some special heat lamps, depending on the temperature range in your home.

Humidity (water in the air) is really important to the veiled chameleon, so you'll need to spray the cage with a mist of water several times a day. This reptile doesn't need a water dish, because it prefers to lick droplets right from leaves. When you're away at school, you can leave a few ice cubes on the screen top, letting it drip onto leaves in the cage. Humidity should stay at about 50%, and you can monitor that by keeping a little humidity gauge in there.

Veiled chameleons eat insects and will consume a few crickets, waxworms, or mealworms each day. They also like to eat veggies, so you can clip collard or mustard greens to the cage for them to chomp on when they feel like it. Clean out the cage frequently to keep mold from growing.

THIS PET'S IN COLOR-RAMA!

Adult veiled chameleons change their colors and patterns depending on light, temperature, and mood. Generally, dark colors mean they are stressed or cold,

while bright colors indicate a happy or active chameleon. Males are brighter than females, but both can colorize themselves with shades of yellow, green, blue-green, turquoise, brownish-reds, and black.

To make this happen, they have a bunch of layers of skin cells, and each layer does different things. Upper layers have color cells that are yellow and red, and can change size. So, if the chameleon is feeling yellow, it can make the yellow cells bigger, and we see big yellow patches on the skin.

Under the color layers, there are cells that can reflect blue light. When blue light is reflected and sent up through the layer of color cells, the colors mix. If the blue goes through yellow, for instance, we see green. The shades are different, depending on how much blue light is reflected.

The cells in the bottom skin layer are shaped sort of like a squid, with tentacles that reach up through the other layers of skin. In these cells there is something called melanin, which the chameleon moves around into different places in the cells. If the melanin is pushed up to the end of the tentacles at the surface of the skin, then that part of the reptile looks very dark. If the melanin stays deep down, that part of the skin stays bright. There are lots of patterns of stripes and spots that these cells can make, depending on how much melanin is moving around.

VARIOUS INTERESTING THINGS ABOUT CHAMELEONS...

WHEN UNDER ATTACK, TURN BLACK

If a veiled chameleon feels threatened, sometimes it will turn very dark brown or black and play dead to fool the predator. When cold, chameleons also change to very dark colors to absorb heat better.

KEEP YOUR EYE ON THAT TONGUE!

A veiled chameleon has a sticky tongue that's $1^1/_2$ times longer than its body. The end of the tongue is thicker than the base, and it shoots out and back in a split second, using suction to capture its prey.

HEY, DUDE! OR DUDETTE?

Male chameleons are longer than females, but thinner. You can also tell a male by looking at the casque (helmet-like ridge on top of the head). A male's casque is larger than a female's, and can reach two inches (5 cm) in height. Another way to I.D. a male is to look for a flap of flesh, or "tarsal spur," on the rear feet.

LET'S GET LARGE...

Veiled chameleons can puff themselves up to scare away attackers, or to increase their surface area to absorb more of the Sun's rays. When they do this, they look really big from the side, but when you look at their bodies from the head or tail view, they are really, really flat.

LEAF ME ALONE!

These guys are well adapted to living in trees. Their bodies are leaf-shaped, and they can sit for long periods of time waiting for prey to come within reach. When they walk along a branch, they move very slowly, swaying from side to side, like a leaf in the breeze.

WHAT ARE YOU LOOKIN' AT?

The eyes on this chameleon stick out from the head and can move in separate directions, allowing it to see in front and back at the same time. When getting ready to eat, though, it will focus both eyes on the prey in order to see depth. Unlike many reptiles, veiled chameleons can see color, too.

IS THAT A THIRD EYE?

There is a small, light-sensitive spot on top of the head. It doesn't form an image, but it does act sort of like an eye by perceiving violet and blue light.

HOW IS A CHAMELEON LIKE A MONKEY?

Veiled chameleons are zygodactyls (have opposable toes on their feet) so they can grip branches really well. This is very much like the opposable thumb that primates have. This chameleon also has a prehensile tail, which means it curls and grasps like a monkey's.

ASK THE PET WHIZ

Q: I heard that if you put a chameleon on plaid, it will go crazy and die. Is this true?
A: In a word: NO. Chameleon skin can only make certain colors and patterns, and it doesn't change to match backgrounds. Yes, chameleons can camouflage themselves, but only in their natural habitats.

Q: Can I train my veiled chameleon to come when I call him?
A: Not likely. These reptiles are practically deaf. They have such tiny ear holes that you can't even see them. They really only hear vibrations and some tones.

Q: Are these chameleons friendly?
A: Veiled chameleons are considered to be asocial, which—according to *Webster's Dictionary*—means they are selfish and inconsiderate of others. They don't like living with other chameleons and will even get kind of nasty if they see their own reflections. Unfortunately, they aren't thrilled with any other animals, either—including humans. If you get one young, and hold it frequently, you might be able to train it to like you. But most veiled chameleons don't like being held, and they do have teeth. This, guys, is a pet that's really a visual experience.

BEARDED DRAGON

IF you've always dreamed of having a dragon for a pet, it's time to wake up and smell the mealworms! This EXCELLENT lizard loves human friends, likes being carried around, and will even communicate with you via dragonese. Of course, it's also ugly, expensive, and messy, but, HEY, it doesn't breathe fire!

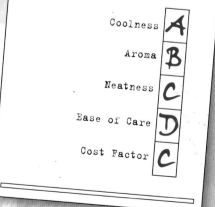

THE DRAGON LAIR

A baby beardy can live in a 10-gallon (38-liter) tank, but within a year it will need something much bigger. An adult should have a 40-gallon (151-liter) tank, and if you have more than one dragon, you'll need a 50-gallon (189-liter) at least. A screen top is a must, and thick branches should be put in the tank for basking. You'll also want a hide box in there.

The bearded dragon needs a basking light on for about 12 hours a day to provide UVB rays. In the daytime, temperatures in the tank need to stay at about 100°F (38°C) in the basking spot, and 75° to 85°F (24° to 29°C) in the rest of the tank. At night it can dip to about 70°F (21°C). Some combination of lights, under-tank heaters, and timers will be needed to keep temps in the right ranges.

You'll have to clean up the tank frequently, because this reptile has a large appetite and a fast metabolism. (Translation: Poop production is high.)

Report Card

Coolness	A
Aroma	B
Neatness	C
Ease of Care	D
Cost Factor	C

THE DRAGON DIET

Bearded dragons are omnivores, which means they'll eat just about anything. An adult will likely go through about a dozen bugs (crickets are best) every other day and will also eat bunches of veggies. Greens are really important (kale, collard, and mustard greens), as well as squash, yams, carrots, and fruits.

Your beardy might want to drink water from a dish, but most don't. They seem to get all the water they need from their food, but they also might lap up some water if you mist the tank every once in a while with a spray bottle. Young dragons have greater water needs than adults.

NICE DRAGON!

Bearded dragons are usually great with people. They are diurnal (active during the day), and since (most) humans are also diurnal, there are a lot of opportunities for quality time. Beardies are happy being handled, as long as you scoop them up gently and support their tails. (They get all off balance if their tails are flopping around.) Lots of dragon owners carry them around on their shoulders.

Bearded dragons also like other bearded dragons, as long as their living space is big enough. If you have more than one beardy, it's important that they are about the same size. If one is too much bigger than the other, the big one might like the little one so much that it will eat it. You also might find it a mistake to have a male and a female together, since they will like each other so much that you will soon be taking care of a whole bunch of baby dragons.

SPEAKING DRAGON

Beardies are alert and curious and communicate with people in some of the same ways they communicate with other beardies. Circular waving of a hand (well, forelimb) means they want to be your friend. Head-bobbing means they want to mate with you (or that they want you to go away—it's

hard to tell). If you make these same kinds of motions to them with your fingers, they will think you're telling them those same things.

When a beardy is REALLY trying to impress or scare another beardy, it will "display," or puff up its spiky throat pouch (the "beard"). When the beard turns black, and is accompanied by head-bobbing, mouth-gaping, and a flattened body, the dragon is SERIOUSLY into it, and it's definitely NOT time to pick it up.

SCI-NAME: *Pogona vitticeps*
LENGTH (head to tip of tail): 13–24 in. (33–61 cm)
LIFESPAN: 4 to 10 years

ASK THE PET WHIZ

Q: Is it just the male that has the throat pouch?

A: Nope. In the land of dragons there are bearded ladies, too. They don't display as much as males, though.

Q: My bearded dragon won't let me pick him up. How do I get him to trust me?

A: One word: waxworms. Beardies are suckers for these things, and you can get them at most pet stores. Just put one in your hand, and he'll be crawling into it in seconds!

Q: Can I let my bearded dragon out of its tank to walk around?

A: If you have a basking light it can reach, and if you don't mind cleaning up little piles of dragon poop, then the answer is YES.

Q: I want to keep my bearded dragon tank in my room. Will it make noise and keep me up at night?

A: Raise your hand if you've ever had a hamster that ran in one place all night long until you got so cranky you picked up its squeaky wheel and threw it out the window (hopefully without the hamster in it). Well, you'll be happy to know that bearded dragons do NOT do this. In fact, they fall asleep almost as soon as the lights are turned off at night.

Q: Do bearded dragons bite?

A: Sometimes, but they display the beard first, which gives you a pretty obvious warning.

Q: Do they have sharp claws?

A: Yes, and you will DEFINITELY want to clip them now and then if you handle your dragon. Though this may sound hard, it's not. You just set your beardy on your lap, and lift up one foot at a time, and clip off the black tips of the claws. They just kind of sit there and let you do it—unlike cats, which are known to go BALLISTIC in the same circumstances.

GREEN ANOLE

GREEN when it's not brown, that is! These little lizards are very cool to watch because they can change colors, and they're always performing acrobatics by clinging with their sticky feet to just about anything in their tanks. This is a pretty good reptile for beginners, but it does have a downside—green anoles don't like being held.

DIRECT UV AND OTHER IDEAS FOR A HEALTHY HABITAT

Since green anoles are from warm places, you'll need to turn up the heat for these little guys. Ultraviolet (UV) light is needed for basking, which you can provide with fancy UV lights. Or you can put the tank next to a window and get some free rays direct from the world's main supplier of UV: the Sun. Unless your home is REALLY hot all the time, you will also need an under-tank heater. Putting a cheap, stick-on thermometer in the tank will help you keep the temps in the right zone: 78° to 85°F (26° to 29°C) during the day and 60° to 70°F (16° to 21°C) at night.

You can keep your green anole in a 10-gallon (38-liter) aquarium tank. Cover the bottom with bark (the best is orchid bark, available in pet stores), and set a couple of leafy, potted plants in there. You'll need to water the plants regularly, and also spray a fine mist of water onto the leaves a couple of times a day. This is because anoles lick the water droplets right from the leaves to stay hydrated (filled with water, sort of). Clean-up is really easy—just pull out dirty pieces of bark every few days.

SCI-NAME: *Anolis carolinensis*

SIZE: 5–8 in. (13–20 cm)

LIFESPAN: 4 to 8 years

Report Card

The
Green Guy

Coolness	C
Aroma	A
Neatness	A
Ease of Care	A
Cost Factor	B

WATCH OUT FOR KILLER CRICKETS, AND OTHER THOUGHTS ON FEEDING

Green anoles are carnivores —insectivores, to be more specific. Crickets or mealworms work just fine, dusted occasionally with a multivitamin/D3 powder (available at pet stores). It's important to get small insects, because—unlike snakes —these reptiles will not eat something larger than their heads. In fact, if left too long with large, hungry crickets, your anole can actually become the prey. (NOT a pretty picture.)

As far as water goes, since the anoles are licking droplets off leaves, you don't need to provide a water dish. They would probably ignore it anyway, because anoles seem to need the drip-drip sound in order to know water is there.

Interesting facts...

Green anoles are diurnal. This means they are active in the day, and they sleep at night.

Anole toe pads are covered with little hairs, which help them cling to things –including the glass walls of the tank.

Like the gecko, a green anole has autotomic powers–it can lose its tail and grow it back.

Green anoles are mute–they don't make any sounds at all.

Anoles change colors depending on their moods. Generally, the greener they are, the happier and more active they are. They turn shades of brown when they are sleeping or cold, or when they are scared or sick.

In the wild, green anoles can grow to 12 inches (30cm) long.

Q: Can I have more than one anole in the same tank?
A: You can have a bunch of anoles together, but the more you have, the bigger the tank you'll need. ALSO, you have to make sure you don't put two males together, because they are known to fight —to the death, even. Which kind of defeats the purpose of having more anoles in the first place, in my opinion.

Continued on page 41

Q: So, males and females get along?

A: Except during mating season, when the male anole spends a lot of time annoying the female anole. Then there is the matter of baby anoles, which are REALLY hard to take care of. For example, you have to feed them insects the size of a pinhead. If you're at all farsighted you won't even be able to see these things. My advice is to stick with females if you want multiple anoles.

Q: How do I tell if an anole is female?

A: Males have a flap of pinkish skin under the throat, called a dewlap (which they fan out very attractively to try to impress females). Of course, sometimes female anoles have dewlaps, too, so this isn't a foolproof way to I.D. anoles. Sometimes you can tell females because they can have white stripes down their backs, but you can't rely on that method, either, because young males have white stripes, too. As you can see, figuring out the sex of an anole is VERY confusing.

Q: Why can't you handle a green anole?

A: They are very afraid of people because to them, we are big, giant, clumsy humanoids. Because of this, when you try to hold an anole it will try to get away from you, and you will likely be left with nothing but the anole's tail in your hand. Also, their feet stick so well to things that their toes can rip right off when you try to pick them up. If holding your reptile is important to you, I recommend you get a leopard gecko or a corn snake.

REPTILE WRAP-UP!

OR...WHAT ELSE YOU NEED TO KNOW
ABOUT YOUR ECTOTHERM

DON'T KISS THAT REPTILE!

Reptiles sometimes carry salmonella bacteria, which doesn't make them sick, but can make people really ill (especially babies and people with health problems). SO, it's important that you wash your hands after handling any scaly pets. Keeping a big bottle of waterless hand disinfectant next to the tank makes this very easy. Scoop out feces (poop) often, and dispose in a plastic bag, like you do with dog poop. Tank cleanings should never be done in places where people eat or brush their teeth, and you should use gloves and sponges that can be tossed out after each cleaning. Disinfecting the tank with a mild bleach solution kills bacteria. GET AN ADULT TO HELP WITH THE TANK CLEANINGS, BECAUSE IT CAN BE HARD!

DIY CRICKETS AND MEALWORMS...

If you get a reptile that eats insects, you'll soon find that you have to buy these bugs at the pet store CONSTANTLY. To save a whole lot of time and money, DIY (That's do-it-yourself!) Raising crickets and mealworms is easy, and you can get step-by-step instructions from kits at pet stores, or from the web.

No matter where your crickets or mealworms come from, it's a good idea to dust them with a multivitamin/ mineral powder before feeding them to your reptile. You can buy it at pet stores, then sprinkle some in a little bag, add a few bugs, and SHAKE! (Gently, though—most reptiles like to eat insects that move.)

1: Are you TOUCHY-FEELY? Do you need a soft, lovable reptile you can hug?

If your answer is YES, then you are obviously a person in need of a corn, king, or milk snake. The scales are soft, and hugging is what constrictors are all about!

If your answer is NO, you're not done yet...

2. Are you SHALLOW? Are looks more important to you than personality?

If your answer is YES, then you have some ISSUES you might want to deal with, my friend. The veiled chameleon is probably a good reptile for you, though. It's all about the visuals and doesn't like others—no matter what they look like!

If NO, keep on keepin' on...

3. Are you a VAMPIRE? Do you need a reptile that is active late at night?

If YES, then the very cool (and NOCTURNAL) leopard gecko is your perfect pet!

Continued on page 45

WHERE DO YOU GET REPTILES? ONE OPTION: MARS!

The best way to find a healthy reptile is through breeders. There are several good networks of reptile breeders, and there are even big shows where you can go meet breeders, see the reptiles, and buy them there. One of these is called MARS (Mid-Atlantic Reptile Show). You can get reptiles at some pet stores, too, but they aren't always really healthy. Sometimes pet stores even sell wild-caught reptiles, which aren't as tame as captive-breds. Also, employees at pet stores are not usually reptile experts, so you won't learn as much about the animal you buy.

TURNING UP THE HEAT ON YOUR REPTILE

Since ectotherms (cold-blooded critters) can't make any heat on their own, the lighting/heating thing is VERY important. Make sure you do your research on the specific needs of your reptile. Ask the breeder, or check out some websites on the particular reptile you choose. (A Google search will get you to lots of sites.) Generally, tropical species are going to have

If NO, then move on down the line…

4. Are you SPACEY? Like, do you sometimes forget you even HAVE a pet?

You should stick to larger reptiles that don't eat (or poop) as frequently: corn, king, and milk snakes are good choices. Keep any lights or heaters on automatic timers, though, and use a large water dish. But try putting some notes around — on your computer, your bathroom mirror — to make you a better pet-owner. (The same method can work for homework, too!)

5. Are you SQUEAMISH? Is there NO WAY you're feeding defenseless, little animals to a reptile?

If YES, then snakes are out of the running, except the rough green snake. If you even feel sorry for the (literally) cold-blooded killing of insects, then you should definitely read on to find an extreme pet that's NOT a reptile.

If NO, then you've reached the end of the quiz, and you are still just as confused. Don't worry, though —there are lots more animals ahead to make you even MORE confused!

more demanding (and expensive) lighting needs than reptiles that live naturally in your climate. Buy a cheap thermometer to stick on the inside of the cage to make sure you've got the temps right.

NOW...ARE YOU READY TO CHOOSE A REPTILE PET?

Or, after reading all this stuff, are you thinking: Chyuh!?

I'm more confused now than I was before! Either way, you may want to analyze your extreme pet psyche (that's sike-ee) with the... PET WHIZ POP QUIZ on page 43!

FERRET

EVER wanted a weasel? Ached for an otter? Imagined a mink flopped luxuriously over your shoulder? Well, my kinda strange friend, today is your lucky pet day! Introducing the SLINKY AND FURRY, SLOPPY AND FLOPPY, STINKY BUT FABULOUS…FERRET!

THE HISTORY OF THE FERRET (AND MAYBE SOME RUMORS)

Legend has it that ferrets were kept as pets in ancient Egypt, maybe as long ago as 1300 B.C., to keep mice and rats away. At some point cats took over the job, apparently. This had to have been a HUGE embarrassment to the ferrets.

Later, ferrets appeared in Rome, and then all over Europe, and became well-

Report Card

Mustela Marks

Coolness	A+
Aroma (if you're clean)	C
Aroma (if you're not)	D
Neatness	C-
Ease of Care	C
Cost Factor	C-

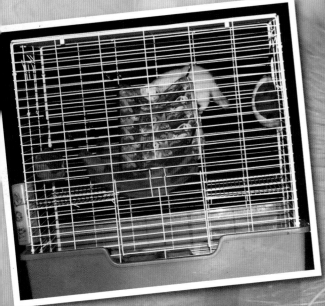

known for "ferreting," or diving into the holes of rabbits. This was a great help to rabbit hunters, who stood, poised, at the other ends of the holes, nets in hand. ("What's in it for the ferret?" you might ask. Answer: FUN!)

Seafaring ferrets were hardworking throughout history, too! Ship captains would load a few in their boats before setting sail to keep rodents from taking over. Considering that ferrets wobble even when walking on firm ground, the sailors must have gotten many hours of amusement watching these little guys stagger around the decks in pursuit of mice.

Ferret service goes beyond land and sea, too! Airplane manufacturers have used our furry friends to run wires through tight spaces in aircraft assemblies.

In 1875, Queen Victoria of England kept ferrets as pets. (This can be a good point to bring up when you're trying to talk your mother into getting a ferret. Start by saying, "Mom, you deserve to have all the things a QUEEN has.")

SCI-NAME: *Mustela furo*

SIZE: Males (or "gibs") can get as big as 2 feet (.6 m) long and up to 5 lbs (2.3 kg) in weight. As with humans, the male ferret is messier than the female, eats more, and when he wakes up he stares blankly into space for a while.

Females (or "sprites") are a little shorter and usually don't get heavier than 3 lbs (1.4 kg). Females are more alert and restless than males, respond to high-pitched, squeaky sounds, and like to play with little toys.

LIFESPAN: 8 to 9 years, sometimes longer. Basically, a ferret year is equal to about 11 human years.

Ferrets were first raised in the U.S. in the 1930s or 1940s for farmers to keep in their yards for rodent and rabbit control. In the 1970s — once someone figured out how to remove the scent glands — ferrets became popular as pets.

Recently, ferret-lovers in California tried to get Governor Arnold Schwarzenegger to decriminalize ferret-owning. His response: "I love ferrets. I costarred with a ferret in *Kindergarten Cop.*" But he hasn't changed the law. Perhaps he's friends with actor Ben Stiller, who hates ferrets because he got bitten by one on his chin during the filming of *Along Came Polly.*

The cage should be set up with a litter box on the bottom, food and water on a different level, and a hammock hanging from the top. You should cover the shelves of the cage with old rags and clothes, because your ferret will like to burrow in these. Also, it kind of reminds the ferret to only "go" in the litter box, because they usually won't mess up their bedding like that.

Ferrets need to spend at least a couple of hours out of their cages every day. On a nice day, this can be outside (with you watching), but on really hot or cold days, they need a place to run around indoors. Keep the following in mind when picking a spot in your home:

Ferrets are really messy. They'll poop all over the floor (usually in corners) if you don't watch them carefully. Put some litter boxes out in the play area, and train your ferret to use them. You can get good housebreaking tips from books and websites, but you still shouldn't choose your dad's antique Persian rug for your ferret to run around on.

They can crawl into really tight spaces, which can be dangerous when it's the back of a washing machine or a refrigerator. Think like a ferret when deciding if a room is safe.

Very young ferrets bite and chew on stuff because their teeth are growing in. This can include your fingers (MAJOR OUCH) and objects like your sneakers, headphones, or computer cords. Until they get over this—at about four months of age—this will have a lot to do with where you can let them play.

You don't have to bathe a ferret very often. Some people do it every few weeks, others every few months. Bathing outside, on warm days, is the most entertaining. Get a small kiddie or doggie swimming pool, and fill it with warm water until there are about four inches (10 cm) of water in there. Watch your ferret swim around for a while, and when you get bored with that, put some shampoo on a washcloth and scrub away. Ferrets are usually calm during baths, and they look really cute with bubbles all over them. Rinse well and rub him dry with a towel, then let him crawl around in a pile of dry towels.

Claw clipping and ear cleaning are more difficult tasks, but really important. To do the clipping, hold a paw in one hand, and clip the tip of the claw, being careful not to clip the pink part—that hurts! To clean the ears, follow directions on the ear cleaner you get. They will hate this as much as the claw clipping. HINT: Attempt these things when your ferret is sleeping. By the time she wakes up, you should be at least halfway done, and then you can do the rest next time she's asleep.

OWNING AND OPERATING YOUR FERRET

The Basic Equipment:

Large, wire cage with at least two levels

Hammock (for the ferret, not for you)

Litter boxes (big enough for your ferret to stretch out in)

Recycled paper litter

Large hanging water bottle

Heavy food dish or type that attaches to side of cage

Dry ferret food

Ferret shampoo or no-tears baby shampoo

Ear cleaner

Claw clipper

Lots of old towels, T-shirts, and other rags to use for bedding

ASK THE PET WHIZ

Q: I've heard that ferrets really reek. Is this true?

A: Ferrets in the pet trade have had scent glands removed, but there is still some B.O. going on. If it were a bottled fragrance it might be advertised like this: Eau de Ferret —an earthy stroll down a forest path, with just a slight whiff of week-old skunk. Ferret-lovers say it's "woodsy." But the really major odorama that goes on with ferrets is the stench of a litter box that hasn't been emptied. If you clean up a lot, then it's not so bad.

Continued on page 53

Speaking ferret and other tips for playing with your pet...

Ferrets LIVE for TOWEL RIDES! Put a towel on the floor and set your ferret on top of it. Take the other end and pull him around the floor!

SNAKE is an excellent ferret game. Take some pairs of old jeans, cut off the legs, and spread them around on the floor. Your ferret will have an awesome time tunneling through! Try using sweatpants and the sleeves of sweatshirts for some variety. (Great way to recycle those old clothes!)

Ferrets seem to have an ON-OFF switch. They are either in OUT-COLD-ASLEEP MODE, which can go on for about 15 hours a day; OR they are in BOING-INTO-WALLS-WITH-JOY MODE, which happens whenever they spot someone to have fun with. Namely: YOU.

DOOK-DOOK, CHIP-CHIP, ER-ER-ER are some of the sounds your ferret might make when he is playing. These are happy sounds, and if you want to talk to your ferret, you can use these same noises. (Of course, you run the risk of actually saying something you don't mean in ferret-ese, such as "I LOVE it when you pee on my shoes!")

There are many other great ways a ferret can TOTAL THE HOUSE. Some suggestions: Give your ferret a roll of toilet paper, a ball of yarn, or mass quantities of plastic grocery bags. She will GO CRAZY! Of course, there will be some clean-up involved, but if you're getting a ferret, you better get used to the whole concept of "clean-up."

Here is a game called WADS OF FUN: Take a stack of used papers – your math notebook from last year might be an especially satisfying source – and wad up each sheet into a ball. Toss them gently at and around your ferret. You will soon have a ridiculously happy and overexcited ferret leaping and scooting around the room.

DANCING is a major ferret activity. A ferret who wants to dance will choose a partner (you) and tug (you) by the feet onto the dance floor. Ferrets tug like dogs – that is, with teeth – so you should consider stocking up (hehe!) on thick socks, because a nip from an over excited, dance-crazed ferret can hurt. No music required.

ASK THE PET WHIZ

Q: Should I let my baby brother play with my ferret?
A: No. Ferrets are not for young kids. They don't understand ferrets, so they can get bitten, and a whole of screaming will be going on.

Q: Are there any tricks I can teach my ferret?
A: You can teach your ferret to come to a sound, like a particular squeaky toy. Give him a treat (a raisin, small piece of apple, a good head-scratching) whenever you squeak the toy, and after a while, he'll come runnin' when he hears it. Also, you can teach your ferret to stay up on your shoulder. Stand on something soft, like a mattress, and put your ferret on your shoulder. Every time she falls off, say NO! and pick her up and put her back on. Whenever she stays there for a while, give her a treat. Start training when your ferret is young, and do it every day until she gets it.

Q: Is it a good idea to have two ferrets?
A: If you can, yes. When you get two young ferrets, they grow up very happy. They always have a friend to play with, even when you have too much homework, or you're on a ski trip, or you're just not in a playing mood. And watching two ferrets play is really amusing – it's like a cartoon.

Q: Do all ferrets look alike?
A: No. Just like cats and dogs, there are a bunch of different breeds of ferrets. A SABLE has a lot of dark browns in the fur, an ALBINO is all white, a CINNAMON is kind of reddish, a PANDA is black with a white head, and there are more, too.

WHAT PET HAS BEADY BLACK EYES,
A LONG WIGGLY NOSE, AND LOOKS LIKE THE
CHILD OF MR. HAIRBRUSH AND MS. BASKETBALL?
TWO POINTS IF YOUR GUESS IS...

HEDGEHOG!

COMMONLY called the AFRICAN PYGMY HEDGEHOG, these little guys are quiet, timid, and really easy to care for. Though they are naturally nocturnal, they can adapt to your schedule pretty well. There is no noticeable odor (unless you don't clean up after them), and they're cute, in a strange sort of way.

Report Card

Coolness	B+
Aroma	A-
Neatness	B
Ease of Care	A-
Cost Factor	C

HOLDING HAPPY HEDGIES

Get your hedgie when he is young—
6 to 8 weeks is best. This way he will
bond to you for life. Hold him often,
and gently. The underbelly of a hedgie
is extremely soft and fuzzy, but the
rest of him is all spines, or quills, so it
takes some getting used to. You might
want to use a towel at first. Tip: Don't
hold a hedgehog who is trying to sleep
—he'll be grumpy.

SPINE LANGUAGE

Unlike the porcupine, the hedgehog's
quills are not barbed weapons that
can be shot out of its body when it's
mad. (Which might be a cool thing
to watch, but you wouldn't want it
happening in the corner of
your bedroom while
you're sleeping.)
What a hedgehog
does with his
spines, though,
will tell you
how he's
feeling. If
the quills
are lying flat
and smooth,
he's calm
and comfy.
If quills

are sticking up around his face, he's
getting a little worried. If they're
poking out all over his body —
electric-shock-style — then fear
has set in. When he reaches total-
freak-out scared, he will turn himself
into a…

HEDGEBALL!

And THIS is the most awesome thing
about this pet. A hedgehog has a large
muscle running along its stomach
which pulls its body into a tight,
spiked-out ball when it feels it can no
longer face the world. The tail, head,
and feet COMPLETELY disappear
into the ball. Warning: Don't let
your hedgehog morph into a ball over
your finger, because it HURTS. To
make your hedgie come
out of her ball, hold
her in the palm of
your hand, and
gently bounce
her between
palms,
being
ULTRA
careful
not to
drop her.
(Sounds
weird, but it
works.)

SCI-NAME:	*Atelerix albiventris*
SIZE:	5–9 in. (13–23cm) long; ½–1¼ lb. (.2–.6kg) (about the size of a guinea pig)
LIFESPAN:	Usually 4 to 6 years

A HOME A HEDGEHOG IS SURE TO DIG

Put your hedgehog's home in a warm, well-lit area (not direct sunlight, though) that is free of drafts. She will need temps between 65° and 85°F (18°–29°C), so you might have to get an under-tank heater for really cold nights.

Cover the bottom of the tank with at least two inches (5 cm) of bedding—your hedgie will love digging around in it. The litter box should go in a corner, and the food and water as far from it as possible. In addition to the hide box, you can also add a hedgehog wheel (not a hamster wheel—the hedgie can get stuck in it) or other toys. Make sure there is room for the sandpaper ramp, though, because it will keep your hedgehog's nails from getting too long. (You'll probably have to make the ramp.)

THE BASIC EQUIPMENT:

Glass aquarium tank (20-gallon or 76-liter, at least) with a locking screen top or hedgehog cage

Bedding (not cedar)

Small, heavy food dish

Water bottle

Litter box (approx. 6 X 9 in. or 15 X 23 cm)

Non-clumping, dust-free cat litter

Dry hedgehog food, plus some mealworms for treats

Hide box (shoe box or other object, with a door cut in the side)

A ramp covered with sandpaper

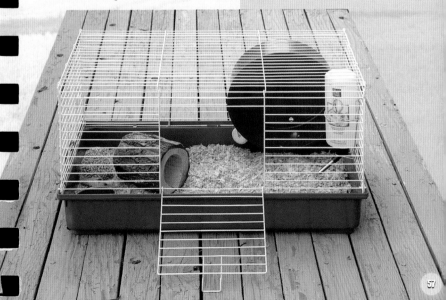

ASK THE PET WHIZ

Q: Do hedgehogs get lonely without other hedgehogs?
A: No. Even though they are easygoing and peaceful, hedgehogs are actually antisocial. They don't like being with any other animals, including humans. (Your hedgie puts up with you because you feed it and let it run around.)

Q: Is my hedgehog sick? He foams at the mouth and covers himself with spit.
A: Your hedgehog is not sick. He's doing something called "self-anointing." When a hedgie comes across a thing that smells a certain way, he licks it until mass quantities of bubbles form in his mouth. Then he takes his long tongue and spreads the saliva all over his quills.

It's strange, sort of gross, and no one really knows why it happens. Probably to give a message to predators or cute hedgehogs of the opposite sex.

Q: My hedgehog poops whenever I pick it up. Is this a problem?
A: For most people, yes, that would be a problem, but I can't speak for you, specifically. Pooping at pickup is not uncommon—it's something that hedgehogs just do (so to speak). Put him in the litter box whenever it happens, and that might help.

Q: I think my hedgehog is a gifted athlete. Are there any sports competitions for hedgehogs?
A: As weird as your question is, the answer is even weirder: YES. There is an International Hedgehog Olympic Gymboree, or IHOG. Some of the events in which your hedgehog can compete include the shot put, floor exercise, hurdles, and the "garden slalom." Some IHOGs include shows, costume competitions, hedgehog portraits, and carnivals.

CHINCHILLA

CENTURIES ago, the chinchilla was the "it" animal for princes and princesses. EVERY royal kid HAD to have one! Of course, they used them as collars for their robes, but that's probably just because they never got to HOLD one of these adorable furballs. (Okay, maybe they STILL would have wanted to wear them. But, HEY, the ancient royals weren't as evolved as we are today. And they didn't have faux fur.)

By the early 1900s, the Chilean government passed laws to stop chinchilla killing and save the animal from extinction. In 1918, a Californian named Mathias Chapman saw his first chinchilla while working in the Andes. He decided to raise them in the U.S. and hired 23 men to go with him into the mountains on a chinchilla-capturing mission. After years of searching, the band of chinchilla hunters caught 11 animals. It took them another year to hike down the mountain. Chapman transported them to California by boat and began to breed them (the chinchillas, not the hunters). Now thousands of ranches raise chinchillas for the pet and fur trade. All chinchillas in the U.S. are descendants of Chapman's original 11 animals.

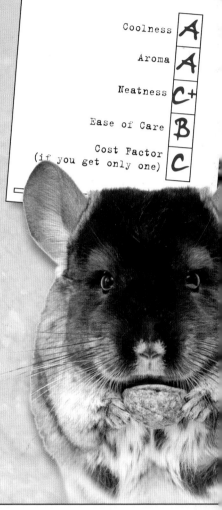

Report Card

Coolness	A
Aroma	A
Neatness	C+
Ease of Care	B
Cost Factor (if you get only one)	C

SCI-NAME: *Chinchilla lanigera*

SIZE: Body is 9–15 in. (23–38 cm) long; tail is 3–6 in. (8–15 cm) long.
Weight: 18–28 ounces (510–794 g). Females are larger than males.

LIFESPAN: 15 to 20 years, in captivity (8 to 10 years in the wild)

While wild chinchillas in the Andes remain endangered and attempts to release ranch-raised chinchillas into their natural habitats are unsuccessful, life is much better in the 21st century. ANYONE can have a living, breathing chinchilla —the SOFTEST animal in the world! They're easygoing, funny, and they have almost no odor. AND — this is a biggie for those of us who can't stop sneezing around those furry animals we love—most people are not allergic to chinchillas. THIS is a FAB pet!

CHINCHILLA DEFENSES (OR...NOT BY THE HAIR OF A CHINNIE-CHIN-CHIN!)

Chinchillas have some pretty cool defense mechanisms. For one thing, they can shoot six feet into the air — like one of those spring toys with the suction cups — to escape from predators. But when unable to jump—as in the case of being actually IN a hungry animal's mouth—chinchillas have a second line of defense: They can let loose wads of fur. This little action can result in a chinchilla (with a bald spot) hopping gleefully off, leaving in its dust a predator angrily swatting its fur-covered tongue. A chinnie's fur also saves him from annoying animals of a much smaller magnitude—fleas and other parasites—because it is so thick that bugs just give up and go away. (To give you an idea of thickness, in the human head there is one hair per follicle; chinchillas have 60 hairs per follicle!)

SETTING UP THE CHINCHILLA CHAMBERS

Put the cage in a quiet spot, so your chinchilla can sleep during the day. Keep the cage out of direct sunlight (they are nocturnal and have no need for Sun), and in a cool part of your home. Temps have to stay below 77°F (25°C) for chinchillas, or you'll need to put a bowl of ice in the cage to cool things off. If the cage is not on a stand,

THE PET CHINCHILLA SHOPPING LIST

Large wire cage, with shelves and ramps - not plastic (Tall cage is best, with minimum 24x24 in (61 X 61 cm) floor space; or a rabbit hutch can work.)

Chinchilla pellets

Timothy hay

Hanging feeders/hoppers (that can't be tipped)

Water bottle (if plastic, must have a chew guard)

Bedding (not cedar or pine)

Treats
You can get packaged chinchilla treats, or try dried banana chips, apple slices, raisins, plain shredded wheat, blueberries, grapes, cranberries, dry oatmeal, and raw pumpkin seeds.

Branches for gnawing - from apple tree, maple, or birch

Chew toys from pet store - chinchilla blocks (pumice), rope and wood toys from chinchilla, parrot, rabbit, or rodent aisles

Hide box or tube

Large exercise wheel with solid surface

Heavy bowl that doesn't tip, larger than the chinchilla

Fine sand (available with chinchilla supplies in a pet store or online)

try to find a table to put it on, because chinchillas get scared when a giant (uh, YOU) hovers over them. Your room is probably not a good place for your chinnie's cage, since nocturnal noisiness can keep a person awake. If you really want him in there, though, ask your parents to get you some earplugs to wear to bed.

You can make things pretty busy in the cage so your pet has lots of stuff to play with. If it's too crowded, rotate things, or save some toys for playtime out of the cage. You'll figure out what she likes and doesn't like. Chinchillas need to chew—in order to keep their teeth from growing too long—so make sure there are always good chew toys or branches around. There shouldn't be any plastic or fabrics in the cage – these things, when chewed, can hurt your chinnie.

CHOW-TIME & OTHER CHINCHILLA CHORES

In the wild, chinchillas eat roots, fruits, leaves, and bark. At your house, you can feed your chinchilla dry pellets and timothy hay, available at pet stores. It's really cute to watch them eat—they sit up and hold the food in their little "hands." Feeding in the evening is best, since that is their active time. Any changes in diet need to be done very gradually. Make sure there is always fresh water available. Food dishes, hay hoppers, and water bottles that attach to the sides of the cage are best, so the chinnie doesn't dump things over or poop in his food and water.

Like rabbits, chinchillas poop all the time, as if they haven't a clue it's going on. Luckily, it's small and dry and easy to sweep up when your chinnie is hopping around outside the cage. They rarely will pee outside the cage. Inside the cage, you need to clean up every day or two to keep things healthy and stink-free. Most of the mess will be in the bedding at the bottom, so it's not so hard to scoop it out and replace it with fresh bedding.

Q: Can I take my chinchilla outside?
A: Sure, but these little guys are REALLY sensitive to heat, so don't do it on hot days. Some chin owners find they can walk them on leashes, but it's not nearly as fun as it sounds. I mean, your chinchilla DEFINITELY won't be prancing along at your heels, and more than likely, you'll look down at some point to find you've been walking an empty leash. (This can be embarrassing when it happens as you pass by a group of neighborhood kids.) I recommend carrying your chinchilla in a pack or pouch instead, since it will most likely want to be sleeping while you're out.

Q: The only chinchilla cage I can find at the local pet store looks kind of small. What's the deal?
A: The deal is, there are some bogus "chinchilla cages" sold at pet stores that are WAY too small. They may be fine for baby chinchillas, but MOST baby chinchillas grow up (said with a hint of "duh"). Check out rabbit or ferret cages—those will work a whole lot better.

Q: I have a little brother who is three years old. Should I let him play with my chinchilla?

Continued on page 67

65

A GOOD NAME FOR A CHINCHILLA: DUSTY

Chinchillas in the wild have always bathed in dust, so you have to create a dust-bath for your chinchilla every day or two. Take a big bowl, fill it with a few inches of fine sand, and put it in the cage. When the chinchilla is ready, he will get in the bowl and go into a major hyper episode, rolling and thrashing all over. This—believe it or not—gets his fur nice and clean. It also covers the surrounding area with sand, so a vacuum cleaner or broom might be a good thing to keep handy.

GETTING CHUMMY WITH YOUR CHINNIE

Taming your chinchilla takes some time and patience. Evening is the best time to work on this, because chinchillas are active then, and not cranky. For the first day or so after you bring her home, leave her alone in the cage so she can get used to the new smells. Hang around near the cage, speaking softly. Slip a treat (a raisin, for instance —chinchillas are MAD for raisins) through the bars when she comes up to sniff you. When the time feels right (or you can't STAND it anymore), open the cage door and put your hand out with a treat in it. Wait until the chinnie feels comfortable getting on your hand, then begin petting her gently, scratching under her chin and behind her ears. When she is good with that, you can cup your hands around her and pick her up. Always be gentle, and never grab by the fur—or she will release it to get away. Paying this kind of attention to your chinnie every day will help her bond to you. She may have some days she doesn't want to be handled, but that's okay. Just let her be, and she'll be fine another day.

THINKING OUTSIDE THE CAGE

Once you've tamed your chinchilla, you can let him play out of the cage.

This is tricky, though! Chinnies are rodents, so they chew-chew-chew! Make sure there are no electrical cords or other dangerous or important things within reach of his teeth. No matter how well you chinchilla-proof the place, though, you probably still won't be able to take your eyes off him when he's romping about. Of course, you will be pretty entertained by all his jumping and zooming and his general manic reaction to freedom. No matter how well you watch him, though, the place he runs around in will get kind of wrecked—a corner of the wall might get a few chunks bitten out of it—so don't pick the fanciest room in the house. This will keep you in your parents' good graces, as will sweeping up your pet's poop trails.

A: No. Your chinchilla would most likely be in danger of being hugged to death, and your little brother would be in danger of being bitten by a very freaked-out, somewhat smushed chinchilla.

Q: Are all chinchillas gray?
A: All wild chinchillas are, but some pet chinchillas have been bred so they're different colors: black, brown, white, Afro-violet (light, smooth gray), and sapphire (pinkish sheen). You can get one of these if you want to pay more, but the basic gray-blue chins are plenty cool, and just as soft.

Q: I think the dust-bath thing sounds awesome. Can humans get clean that way?
A: Uh, I don't know.

It's good to give your chinchilla about 20 minutes of run-around time each day, if possible. Lure him back to you with treats so you don't have to scare him by chasing him down.

¡SALVE LAS CHINCHILLAS! (THAT'S "SAVE THE CHINCHILLAS!" IN SPANISH)

Though the trapping frenzy ended over a century ago, wild chinchillas remain an endangered species. In all, 20 million chinchillas were killed in the Andes—a number that's REALLY hard for an animal population to recover from. Making it harder for the chinchillas, illegal trapping still goes on, and some of their habitat is being cleared for other uses.

There are people trying to help, though! Las Chinchillas National Reserve is a park in Chile that protects the natural areas where the wild chinchillas live. There are about 6,000 chinchillas living in the park. And there is a really cool group—Save the Wild Chinchillas—that raises

money to buy and protect land that chinchillas live on. They also go into towns and schools near the chinchilla habitats and teach people about the animal. They give the kids things to help them remember the chinchillas, like pencils that say:

¡SALVE LAS CHINCHILLAS!

Mathias Chapman

SUGAR GLIDER

EVER seen the '80s movie *Gremlins*? There's this kid who gets a really adorable critter (a gremlin), and it comes with some feeding rules that the kid doesn't follow. So the gremlin turns mean and takes over the kid's room and then wrecks the entire town. Well, sugar gliders are sort of like the gremlin in that movie. They've got the same big, round eyes, and they blink at you lovingly from their peaceful napping nooks. But beware! Like the gremlin, this ultra-cute X-pet has some major feeding issues and can **EASILY** take over your life. Read carefully, my friend, before adopting one of these.

HEY! WHO NEEDS A GOOD REPORT CARD WHEN YOU CAN FLY?

They aren't called gliders for nothing! A sugar glider has a flap of skin (a patagium) on each side of his body, spanning between the front and back leg. He spreads these flaps while launching off his hind legs, then volplanes (glides) as far as 150 feet (46m). His long tail holds him steady in flight (like a kite's tail) and is used for steering (like a rudder on a boat). In the wild, he flies from tree to tree this way and can live his whole life

Report Card

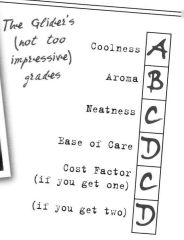

The Glider's
(not too
impressive)
grades

Coolness	A
Aroma	B
Neatness	C
Ease of Care	D
Cost Factor (if you get one)	C
(if you get two)	D

SCI-NAME:	*Petaurus breviceps*
SIZE:	5–8 in. (13–20 cm); with tail, 10–14 in. (25–36 cm) long
LIFESPAN:	10 to 15 years

without ever coming down to Earth! Pet gliders will fly, too—usually when they are with someone they don't know very well, or are sitting in some high place and want to get back to the person they like the most: YOU.

Which leads us to one of the major jobs you'll have as a glider owner. You and your sugar glider have to…

BOND. GLIDER BOND.

Sugar gliders are often called "pocket pets." This is because they are soft and small and will curl up and sleep for hours in your pocket. BUT, you have to bond with them first, and you need to start this as soon as you bring the little guy home. There is a bonding method that seems to work for lots of people, but it may seem kind of strange because it involves, uh, being a tree. You wear a long-sleeved sweatshirt (or T-shirt, if it's too hot to put up with that), and you put a bigger shirt over it. Then you tuck both of those in. (Sweatpants are most comfy for this, even though it looks really stupid. Luckily, you don't have to leave your home for this—or your room, for that matter.) When your sugar glider is active—after sunset, usually—slide him in between the two shirts, and let him climb around on your torso and arms (like he's climbing on a tree

trunk and branches). You can do this for five- or ten-minute intervals, a few times each evening, until he's familiar with your scent and becomes comfy with you. This can take days or months, so you have to keep at it every day until your glider starts to like you.

TIP: Don't get upset with your glider if he doesn't do what you want. Be patient! He'll hold a grudge if you aren't.

ANOTHER TIP: Always give your glider a treat after a bonding session. Probably something sweet is best, but every glider is different.

Which brings us to something else you'll be doing as a glider owner:

BECOMING A SUGAR GLIDER CHEF

In the wild, sugar gliders eat sweet gum from acacia trees, eucalyptus sap, flower nectar, honeydew (that's "excretory product," or turds, from nectar-eating insects), insect larvae, spiders, and lizards. Since your kitchen is—hopefully—not stocked with these

things, and since there is no such thing as a bag of dry sugar glider food, feeding your glider can take up a lot of your time. There are recipes for glider chow that include fruits and veggies, meats, and other foods that don't require a hunting expedition in the rainforest, but expect to do regular shopping and chopping. You may have to try a bunch of different ingredients, too, to find what your sugar glider will eat. They need a balanced diet or they get really sick, so it's best to have a lot of backup from the parentals in order to do this right. But who knows? Maybe this experience will lead to future jobs! You could become a cook at a zoo, or invent the first packaged sugar glider food and make lots of money selling it!

SETTING UP THE GLIDER HABITAT

Your pet store will probably have no supplies specifically designed for sugar gliders AND the people who work there may not even know what they ARE. However, since gliders are pretty, uh, vertical in their habits, you should be able to find lots of the stuff you need in the bird aisle. If that's not working for you, then check out glider websites for links to vendors and ideas for making or finding your own supplies.

STILL READING? HERE'S ANOTHER CHALLENGE FOR YOU:

DIY PROJECT! Make a nesting pouch. Go to a sewing or craft store for pieces of polar fleece—there are lots of great prints and colors to liven up your sugar glider's space.

Pick a spot in your home that is quiet and warm. (Your room is probably a bad choice, since gliders are really active while people sleep. They sometimes even make peculiar barking sounds at night.) If the cage is not on a stand, set it on a table — gliders are into being UP. Put bedding on the bottom of the cage, and attach perches or branches so it's really treelike in there. Hang dishes and the water bottle in the top part of the cage. Nesting pouches should be attached close to the top, too, or set on shelves. If there are no shelves, the exercise wheel will have to go on the bottom. This means you will be cleaning it a lot, since it will be the target of frequent sugar glider bombing raids (if you know what I mean).

GLIDING THROUGH THE DAY WITH YOUR NEW PET

To give you some idea of what your life may be like with a sugar glider, here is what your typical day might look like (for the next 10 years or so):

Morning
Clean all old food out of the cage. Your glider will probably be tired after a long night of eating and playing, so you can keep her in your pocket while you eat breakfast and ransack the house looking for your homework. If you are an especially brain-dead person in the morning and you tend to run into walls or sometimes step into the shower in your pajamas, then just do the morning cleanup and skip the interaction part. (Your glider will thank you.)

Afternoon
Slip your sleeping sugar glider in your pocket while you do your homework, hang out with friends, IM, or whatever. If she wakes up and pokes her head out, pet her and give her a treat — she will probably go back to sleep. She may like to crawl around on you, or snuggle up into your hair. (It's fun to go out and mingle in crowds of strangers when this happens — see if anyone compliments you on your unique hair ornament.)

Evening
When your glider is fully awake, put her in the cage and get her food ready. Make sure she always has fresh water—very important! After she's eaten, you can play with her and let her fly around. Before you go to bed, clean up any messy spots in the cage, and put her in there for a night of nocturnal feasting and craziness.

Q: Is it okay to have two sugar gliders together?

A: It's more than okay — your sugar glider will be TONS happier if you do this. Of course, it costs more. One glider can be as much as $200 to buy, so you do the math. They'll live together, though, so there are no extra costs for the cage, and making double helpings of food is not a big deal. Get two gliders of the same sex, unless you want to go into the breeding business.

Q: What room in my house is best for letting my gliders play?

A: In the wild, sugar gliders just let their droppings disappear into the shrubbery below their trees. It's near-impossible to get them out of this mindset, so think MESSY when picking an indoor play space. Like NOT the room with your mother's brand-new, white couch and matching wall-to-wall carpet.

Q: I don't have any pockets. What do I do?

A: Sad. Very sad. You can use a pouch for your pocket pet, though. This can be something you make, or you can get one of those waist-packs used for biking. There are also glider front-packs available online.

Continued on page 77

GLIDER FACTOIDS...

Some sugar gliders never become tame,
no matter what you do.

Though they are very healthy animals (if fed right),
if you ever need a vet you might have to travel long
distances to find one familiar with sugar gliders.

The way this animal flies is very similar
to the gliding of a paper airplane.

The sugar glider is, technically, an opossum.

For extra fun, add some sound effects to glider playtime by putting in a CD of rainforest sounds!

Glider fur is silky smooth and grayish-blue. There is a dark stripe that runs from the nose, over the head, and straight down the back. There are also stripes near the eyes. In the wild, gliders turn a uniform cocoa brown because of the tree sap and vegetation in their nests. (The original colors come back when they shed.)

A sugar glider is a marsupial, which means the females have pouches to carry their young. Baby sugar gliders are called "joeys" and live in the pouches for about 70 days after birth.

ASK THE PET WHIZ

Another suggestion is to borrow one of your father's big, soft flannel shirts, and wear that around when you're hanging out with your glider. (Your dad will probably be glad to give the shirt to you, at least once he's discovered that a furry animal has been living in the pocket.)

Q: My sugar glider has really sharp nails—OUCH! What can I do about this?
A: You can try putting a sandpaper perch in the cage to help wear them down—these perches are sold for birds. Or, you can clip the nails. (Good luck with that.)

Q: Are gliders legal in my state?
A: Since I don't know where you live, it's a little hard to say. They're wild animals, so check with your state's wildlife agency.

RATS!

WHEN some people (say, parents or teachers) hear the word "rat," they think vile, plague-infested, sewer-dwelling, lice-covered vermin. Though some of you may be thinking, "THAT WOULD BE AN AWESOME PET!" domestic rats are not like that at all. From years of careful breeding, pet rats are actually intelligent, social, entertaining, and clean!

Report Card

Coolness	A-
Aroma	B
Neatness	B+
Ease of Care	A
Cost Factor	A

ONCE UPON A TIME, A RAT'S LIFE WAS THE PITS

This is a really unfortunate tale, but it marks the beginning of RATS AS WE KNOW THEM, so it shall be told.

A few hundred years ago, in London, several rats arrived in a boat from Norway and settled in the streets to raise their little rat families. They were very successful. Soon, there were rats EVERYWHERE.

With the plague and all, the humans of London were not having the same sort of luck with their own families. Feeling outnumbered and threatened, they blamed EVERYTHING on the rats — water pollution, illness,

SCI-NAME: *Rattus norvegicus*
SIZE: Body 9–11 in. (23–28 cm), tail 7–9 in. (18–23 cm)
LIFESPAN: 2 to 3 years…EXCELLENT for short-attention-span pet lovers!

bad grades, you name it. So, London officials hired a man named Jack Black to be the "royal rat catcher." They told Jack it was a good, steady job, and that it even came with benefits: He could keep as many of the rats as he liked. To the London officials this was obviously a knee-slapper, but to Jack it was OPPORTUNITY.

Jack would arrive home each evening with his daily take of rats and head out back to a sports arena, of sorts, which he'd set up. It was really a pit (REALLY), with a bad-tempered dog at the bottom, and Jack would dump all the rats in there. People came to watch and to bet on how many rats the dog could kill. Jack made lots of money.

In the midst of this cruel after-hours business, something strange started happening. Jack started paying attention to the rats' personal qualities. When he identified one that was particularly clever, or sweet, or was prettier than the others, he would

keep it as a pet. And soon, Jack Black, London's royal rat catcher, was breeding rats, and this was the start of...

"THE FANCY RAT"

Though the average rat probably finds the term "fancy" a little embarrassing, it is the official name for rats that are bred and sold as pets. The goal is to breed them to meet a "show standard" because — YES, it's TRUE — there are such things as pet shows for rats. They compete in categories such as "biggest," "most laid-back," "most unusual markings," and "best costume" (although that one can't have a whole lot to do with breeding).

GETTING READY FOR RATTY

Rats are happiest with other rat friends around, but it's not a big deal having more than one rat. They don't need a whole lot of room, and they're MUCH cheaper than most other furry animals.

Pick young rats that seem to get along AND are the same sex (or you may find you have to hire a rat-catcher, too). Rats are not tricky to introduce to your home. Let them get used to their cage for a little while, and approach them slowly at first. Pick up your rat by wrapping your hand gently around the chest and supporting the back feet with your other hand. Rats prefer this to being picked up by their tails.

Make sure your rat always has food, water, and a clean cage. Rats HATE it when it's dirty! They will use one corner as a "bathroom," so you should scoop that out daily and add a handful of fresh bedding. Plan on dumping out all the bedding and starting over once a week to keep your rat happy. (The friends who visit you will be happy, too, because your house won't smell like rodent poop.)

BASIC RAT GEAR

Large (at least 20-gallon or 76-liter) aquarium with locking wire mesh lid OR

Wire cage with horizontal bars to allow climbing (Make sure floor and shelves have smaller openings than 1 inch by 1/2 inch (3 cm by 1.3 cm), or little rat legs can get stuck in them.)

Bedding – recycled paper type is best (never cedar or pine) – to go on the bottom

Nesting material – tissues, paper towels, paper for shredding

Nest box – shoe box, flowerpot on side, and PVC pipe

Heavy food dish

Water bottle

Rat food - laboratory pellets or other rat food from pet store

Chew toys (very important to keep teeth from getting too long)

Wide variety of play toys – ladders, ropes, tunnels, TP tubes, sleeves of old sweatshirts, and paper bags.

Solid-surface exercise wheel

There are more than 32 color varieties of fancy rats, including amber, mink, blue, and lilac. Marking types include "hooded," "masked," "Dalmatian," and others. Coat types can be standard (straight), rex (curly), or satin (shiny). There are also some ultra-special breeds, which cost a bit more than the average rat — Dumbo rats (with large, round ears), odd-eyed rats (with one pink and one dark eye), and tailless or hairless rats (though they SHOULD cost less, since they are missing some key rat parts).

TREATING YOUR RAT RIGHT

Rats are lovable — they like to snuggle and be petted. Some even kiss! Rats learn to recognize their owners and come running when they see them. Of course, all this lovin' will happen more quickly if you give them treats. They like lots of fruits and veggies, and other stuff. Basically, if YOU like it, they'll probably like it. (But ix-nay on the dairy food and junk food—especially no chocolate!) If you're into baking, there's a recipe on page 80 that your rat is sure to eat right up! (Ask a parent for help with the oven, of course.)

ASK THE PET WHIZ

Q: Is my room a good place for the rat tank?

A: By nature, rats are nocturnal, but since they've been pets for so long, they've adapted to human schedules pretty well. HOWEVER, they do like to play most of the night! Taking the wheel out when you go to sleep can help. You just have to see what works for you.

Q: Can I let my rats run around the house?

A: If you want your phone cords and running shoes chewed up, yes you can. Rats are rodents, so they CHEW, man! You do need to take them out of their cage, of course, or else they'll get really bored. But you need to watch them carefully.

Q: Do rats bite?

A: No, not unless they are really, really scared. They are the least likely rodent to bite.

Q: Can I teach my rats to do tricks?

A: Yes! They are VERY SMART, my friend! Some people teach them to come to a certain call, or to a name. Some rats will walk tightropes on command. Others will stay in pockets or on shoulders for hours —even, uh, HOLDING it until their owners put them down to, uh, GO.

Q: If they're SO-O smart, can they help me with my schoolwork?

A: Even though it's PRETTY obvious you expected the answer to be NO-O, it's actually YE-ES. You can get better grades if you have a rat or two, or even three or four. Since they're interesting, they make great subjects for reports, AND lots of kids have used rats as part of their science fair projects—by setting up mazes or teaching them tricks.

MORE PETS for YOUR POCKETS

Here are a couple more **WILD** snugglables. Like the sugar glider, these will bond to your scent and hang out in your pockets for **LIFE**!

THE SHORT-TAILED OPOSSUM

Monodelphis domestica is three to six inches (8 to 15 cm) long (plus another few inches of tail), with thick, gray-brown fur. They have pointy snouts and hairless tails that wrap around branches. In the tribal villages of Brazil, they are kept in houses to eat annoying insects and mice. This one can't fly like a sugar glider, but it costs about half as much, will live in a **MUCH** smaller cage, and is **HUGELY** easier to feed!

SOUTHERN FLYING SQUIRREL

Glaucomys volans (a.k.a., American flying squirrel) lives in large numbers in forests of the U.S. and Canada, but most people never lay eyes on these shy furballs. They look a lot like the average squirrel, only they have flying flaps, and they're **TINY**—just three to four inches (8–10 cm) of body plus a fuzzy tail. As a pet, it's pretty much the same deal as caring for a sugar glider, only the southern flying squirrel has a habit of hoarding food (or, **SQUIRRELING** it away), which means you have to clean out the nests all the time, or the cage will quickly change from a squirrel habitat to a mold habitat. No cool racing stripes on this glider, but it's **REALLY** cute!

MADAGASCAN HISSING COCKROACH!

NO, this is **NOT** your common cockroach! You won't find this one lurking under your dog's dish, or slumbering in the towel you left on the bathroom floor. **THIS** cockroach won't be scurrying across your kitchen at night, causing your family to **LEAP** up on countertops! Oh, no, not **THIS** cockroach!

OKAY, OKAY, it **WILL** cause your family to leap up on countertops. (Sorry to almost ruin your fun.)

The **MADAGASCAN HISSING COCKROACH** is, without a doubt, the **COOLEST COCKROACH** on the planet. It's **BIG** and **SLOW**, and it **CRAWLS ALL OVER YOU.**

Life doesn't get much better than this, does it?

COCKROACH CARE

The list:

5- or 10-gallon (19- or 38-liter) tank with tight-fitting lid

Substrate — soil and leaves from outside, or bedding from pet store

Hide spots — cardboard box or egg carton, tree bark, etc.

Sponge

Food — dog or cat kibble

Snacks — oranges, carrots, yams, bananas, or just about anything else you want

You can keep several of these cockroaches together, although you may want to stick to same-sex groupings unless you want to breed them. They are not real fussy about the temperature, but you don't want it to get too cold. You can keep a little dry food in the tank all the time, but clean it out when it gets moldy. The fruits and veggies you put in can get kind of rotten, but when hairy mold starts growing on them, you may want to clean it out. Water can be provided with the sponge, which should be kept wet - set it on a plastic lid to keep it from getting gross. The tank should only need a complete cleaning every few months. Yay!

As you probably guessed, these cockroaches are from the island of Madagascar, off the east coast of Africa. They live in the leaf litter of tropical forests, coming out at night to eat rotten fruit. They are important in nature because they are decomposers, AND because they are a food source for birds, lemurs, and lizards. GO ROACHES!

Hissing cockroaches are dark brown with dark orange markings on the ABDOMEN (or big body part that includes rear end). The abdomen has cool segments that make this bug look sort of like an armadillo. Male cockroaches have blunt horns on the THORAX (or body part that's attached to the head). There are two ANTENNAE (that would be more than one antenna) —the female's antennae are short and point down, while the male's antennae are long and point up.

COCKROACH CONTACT

Pick up by the thorax, carefully and slowly. They have feet that are like Velcro, so you have to slowly pry them off of things, or else their legs fall off. (Which isn't very cool.) These guys will crawl around your hands and arms, and move slowly enough that you probably won't lose them inside your clothes.

SCI-NAME:	*Gromphadorhina portentosa*
SIZE:	2–4 in. (5–10 cm) long; 1 in. (2.5 cm) wide
LIFESPAN:	2 to 5 years, usually

HISSY FITS

Because these cockroaches can't bite, sting, spit venom, or electrocute their predators the way many other arthropods can, they HISS. This happens when air is pushed out of the cockroach's body through small breathing tubes, much the way a bagpipe makes music. (Though many people would argue that the cockroach's sound is more pleasing.) Some predators startle at the HISS, giving the cockroach a chance to escape.

Male cockroaches actually have a few different HISSES in their vocabulary — one to defend territory, one to express fear, and one to impress females. It's thought that the roaches learn to recognize one another by the different qualities of their sounds.

Report Card

Coolness (if you hang out with people who like cockroaches)	A
(if you hang out with people from Earth)	F
Aroma (unless you leave rotting fruit in the tank too long)	A
Neatness	A
Ease of Care	A
Cost Factor (if you get one)	A
(if you get a few)	B

THINGS TO DO WITH ROACHES!

Have you exhausted the thrill of freaking out everyone you know by appearing in public with huge cockroaches roaming your body?

WELL, maybe you could try one of THESE fun activities!

GET UP CLOSE AND PERSONAL

Find a big magnifying glass and CHECK IT OUT. These are AWESOME critters close-up! Look for the hairs on the antennae, check out the compound eyes, see how the legs are segmented.

A-MAZED ROACHES

Create pathways with cardboard or wood, set treats in various spots along the way, and watch your yucky little friends wind their way through! Have races! AND, with a little imagination, this amusing pastime can surely be shaped into a science fair project!

THE ROACH PULL

Want to see how strong your cockroach is? Fashion a little harness out of thread, attach it to a small container (the bottom of a small matchbox, perhaps?), and GENTLY hook it up to your bug. Now add one penny at a time to the box, and see how much your roach can pull!

IT'S BEEN 300 MILLION YEARS, AND YOU HAVEN'T CHANGED A BIT!

Yes, folks, cockroaches are considered to be "living fossils" because they are still pretty much the same as they were in the Carboniferous era!

ROACH RADAR

Roaches know what's going on around them mostly because of their antennae, which are very sensitive to the touch. They can move these around to feel where things are. The antennae of male cockroaches are covered with fine hairs, which can actually SMELL a female cockroach.

ROACH FIGHT!

Male roaches get REALLY aggressive with each other. If you have two males, you will hear them hissing constantly. They butt horns, like goats, and push each other with their abdomens. The winner does a whole lot of hissing, and then usually bites off the loser's antennae.

Q: I found an old aquarium in someone's trash. Is that okay for my hissing cockroaches?
A: We're talking cockroaches, here — they'd be happy living in a sewage dump. So, yes, that'll be fine. If the lid is not really tight fitting, you can slather petroleum jelly around the inside of the tank, near the top. They can't walk on it, so they stay in the tank.

Q: Is it fun to breed these cockroaches?
A: If you are asking this question then the answer is probably YES. To breed them, you need to start with at least a few cockroaches. Do some Googling on roach breeding so you know what you're doing. You can end up with 20 to 50 babies at a time, so you'll need a pretty big tank. OR, you can get a reptile or amphibian, and never have to pay for food for it.

Q: I've heard a cockroach can live even if it loses its head. Is this true?
A: Don't test this out with your pet cockroach, but YES. A beheaded cockroach can continue to live because it has six extra brains—one in each leg. Which sounds a whole lot cleverer than it is. I mean, no matter HOW smart those legs are, they don't have mouths, so the cockroach dies in about a week from starvation.

Continued on page 91

MORE ROACH TRIVIA!

Females only mate one time in their lives.

Cockroach droppings are called "frass."

A cockroach can hold its breath for 40 minutes.

Cockroaches "pass gas" every 15 minutes.

You can't sneak up on a cockroach, because it has two little hairs (cerci) on its rear end that act as motion detectors.

Cockroach blood is white.

Cockroaches can see in red light but can't see in green light.

The hairs on the legs of cockroaches increase their sense of touch.

Cockroach innards are made of whitish goo called FAT BODY.

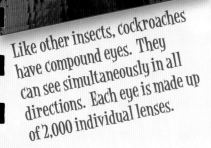

Like other insects, cockroaches have compound eyes. They can see simultaneously in all directions. Each eye is made up of 2,000 individual lenses.

ASK THE PET WHIZ

Q: Is it also true that crushed cockroaches spread on a stinging wound will make the pain go away?
A: AGAIN, I don't recommend you do this with your personal pets, but apparently there is something in cockroach guts that breaks down poisons and gets rid of pain. Which is weird. Probably not as weird, though, as the person who figured that out.

Q: I think my cockroach tank is haunted. The other day I saw a TOTALLY WHITE cockroach in there, and then it was GONE a few hours later!
A: Calm down, now! Chances are you just have a cockroach that is molting. In the first nine months of a cockroach's life, it sheds its skin a bunch of times. This is VERY COOL, because it splits down the top, and the cockroach that crawls out is completely white. Even the antennae are white! Over a couple of hours, it gets dark again.

GIANT
AFRICAN
MILLIPEDE

HAVE you ever wondered if millipedes play an important role in the universe? Lost sleep pondering their function in nutrient recycling? This, my curious friend, may be your lucky day. Rest assured that there must be SOMEONE stranger than you on this vast planet, and sit back, read up, and ALL will soon be revealed.

Millipedes are one of Earth's MAJOR DECOMPOSERS. In forests all over the world, they turn dead plants into nutrients that can be sucked up by tree

Report Card

Coolness (to your buds)	A
Coolness (to the greater planet)	C
Aroma	A
Neatness	A
Ease of Care	A
Cost Factor (if you get one)	A
Cost Factor (if you get more)	B

SCI-NAME: *Archispirostreptus giga*

SIZE: Full-grown, 7 ½–12 in. (19–30 cm) long, and as thick around as your thumb. Very slow-growing, so it can take years to reach full length.

LIFESPAN: 7 to 10 years

roots. Millipedes do this by way of a complicated, highly scientific process, which goes like this: EAT—DIGEST—POOP. That's right: without millipede poop, trees would not grow, and life as we know it would cease to exist.

And, DUDE, these are GNARLY pets!

MILLIPEDES IN THE WILD

Millipedes live all over the planet, but this particular type is from the rainforests of western Africa, where it lives (as most millipedes do) under rocks and in moist dirt and leaves. Millipedes are mainly active at night, chomping away on detritus (dead stuff) with their mandibles (jaws).

As a natural defense against predators, millipedes first roll up into a tight spiral. This protects the head and soft underside. If the

predator continues to persist (and why wouldn't it?), the millipede then releases a foul-smelling and (apparently) gross-tasting toxic fluid from stink glands near their legs.

MILLIPEDES IN THE HAND

Pick up a millipede gently. It will probably coil up at first, but leave it alone in your hand, and it will unwrap itself and start walking around on you. Wash your hands after handling, just in case they release some of the toxin, which can sting if it gets in eyes or a cut. (Millipedes RARELY release this when a

MILLIPEDES IN THE HOME

Since these bugs don't eat each other, you can have more than one millipede living together. YAY!

BASIC MILLI-GEAR:

- 10-gallon (38-liter) plastic or glass tank w/ lid (doesn't have to fit that tight)

- Substrate: 3 - 4 inches (8-10 cm) of peat moss and potting soil

- Pieces of bark for hiding

- Under-tank heater, or heating pad to lay over top

- Spray bottle

- Humidity and temperature gauges

- Calcium powder

Millipedes like it dark, so there is no need for lighting. You should pick a spot that's not too close to a window. Spray the tank with water regularly to keep it moist - at about 75% humidity. Heat should be around 75°F (24°C).

Feed them about every other day with fruits and veggies right from your kitchen! Bananas, melons, tomatos, cukes (a favorite with many millipedes), and anything else you want to try is good. If it's mushy or too rotten for you to eat, then your millipede will like it even better. Dust the food with calcium powder occasionally, so the millipede's exoskeleton stays shiny and healthy. They get all the water they need from the moisture in the tank, and from the food, so you don't need to provide a water dish.

human is holding them. They would need to be super-annoyed, or hurt, before sliming a person.)

millipede has. It's hard to get an exact number, because millipedes can lose legs here and there. Which is not as big a deal for them as it would be for us.

HOW MANY LEGS DOES A MILLIPEDE REALLY HAVE?

The person who was hired to name this bug probably lost his job, because the word "millipede" means, basically, "thousand-legs," and this bug does NOT have a thousand legs. It ONLY has a couple hundred, most of the time. If you want to figure out how many legs your millipede has, here is how you do it:

Count the body segments. (An adult millipede has 40 to 60 body segments.) Multiply this number by 4 (since there are two pairs of legs per segment), and then subtract by 10 (since, on some segments, the "legs" are actually other things that are pretending to be legs, such as hooks for mating). This should result in the approximate number of legs your

MILLIPEDE MISCELLANY (or, random factoids)

Millipedes molt throughout their entire lives, and they need to burrow when they do it. Leave them alone!

ASK THE PET WHIZ

To get calcium, millipedes chew on rocks.

Capuchin monkeys in Venezuela and lemurs in Madagascar have been known to roll millipedes around on the ground until they release their toxins. Then the monkeys rub the gunk into their fur—probably to get rid of mites and fleas. Some monkeys also suck the toxin, which makes them woozy. Not a smart thing to do —especially when you live in a tree.

Millipedes have really bad eyesight. Their compound eyes are not fully developed. They use antennae to help find food.

Q: What is the difference between a centipede and a millipede? I am SO confused!

A: Let me clear this up for you so you can get on with your life. Centipedes have one pair of legs per segment (not two), which come out of the side of the body (not underneath). Centipedes also move faster than millipedes, and in a snakelike way (not straight). Centipedes are also flat and thin, while millipedes are cylindrical.

Although there is some debate among those who have devoted their careers to millipedes, it is commonly thought that the Giant African Millipede is the biggest millipede in the world.

Baby millipedes are coprophagous. (This means they eat the dung of their parents. Yum.)

TARANTULA!

MANY things are said about tarantulas. Such as: "They are usually harmless when treated with respect" and, "Tarantulas have venom, but it's not very toxic."

While these seem like reasonable statements, you are not alone if they raise a few teeny questions in your mind. Such as: "How, exactly, does a tarantula define 'respect'?" or "On a scale of one to ten, how does 'not very toxic' rate?"

If you are thinking of getting a tarantula, READ THIS SECTION CAREFULLY. STUDY THE FACTS like a tarantula studying a cricket. LEAP ON THE INFORMATION the way it would lunge at the insect. DIG YOUR TEETH IN, like fangs boring a hole in the exoskeleton and injecting flesh-dissolving poison. INGEST IT as if sucking up your prey's innards like a smoothie.

Report Card

Coolness	A-
Aroma	A
Neatness	A
Ease of Care	B
Factor	B+

SCI-NAME: *Aphonopelma Chalcodes*

SIZE: Full-grown, 1–5 in. (13–25 cm)

LIFESPAN: 25 to 40 years

BE THE SPIDER. KNOW THE SPIDER. FACTS TO STUDY.

Tarantulas are MONDO, as in BIG. Some have been known to get SO big their legs would hang over the edge of a Frisbee. Tarantulas are also covered with hair, which comes in a variety of colors and patterns, depending on the species (of which there are 800+ worldwide).

Many types of tarantulas are available in the pet trade—some with price tags in the hundreds of dollars—but just a few are considered calm, slow-moving, and inexpensive enough for the beginner. Here are two:

THE CHILEAN ROSE, or *Grammostola gala*—a South American tarantula with a leg span close to six inches (15 cm) and brownish hair that has a pinkish hue and

THE MEXICAN RED-KNEE *Brachypelma smithi* —a Central American species with a five-inch (13-cm) leg span, blackish hair, yellow- or white-striped legs, and red or orange knees.

INFORMATION TO LUNGE AT

A five-gallon (19-liter) aquarium tank is the right size for these tarantulas. If it's bigger, the spider can injure itself falling. Make sure the screen top is very tight-fitting.*

(*In every household in the universe, there is SOMEONE whose worst nightmare is this: A TARANTULA LOOSE IN THE HOUSE. Make sure the lid is REALLY secure, so you are not the reason your family has to abandon its home.)

So your tarantula can burrow, cover the bottom with several inches of soil. Place a shallow water dish somewhere in there, and some sort of shelter —half of a clay pot is good.

Stick cheap temperature and humidity gauges in the tank, because you need to make sure the temps stay at about 75°F (24°C) and the humidity is in the 60–75% range. You may need to use an under-tank heater and spray the tank daily with water to keep the environment right for your hairy friend.

Q: I saw a tarantula at a pet store. Is that a good place to buy one?
A: Only if you are SURE it is the type of tarantula you want. KNOW THE SPECIES. BE AN EXPERT. Don't trust the pet store dude to know about tarantulas (especially if he's got headphones on and just seems to be nodding at everything you say). Lots of people get their tarantulas by ordering online. You know you'll get the right species. Of course, you run other risks. For instance, a tarantula that has been stuffed in a box and shipped by U.S. mail may feel there has been a lack of respect and not be in the best sort of mood when it arrives.

Continued on page 103

A big cricket should be fed to your tarantula about once or twice a week. Take it out if it's not eaten in a day. Tarantulas can go for a month without eating, so it doesn't mean a whole lot if they don't eat every time you feed them.

If you are a person who HATES cleaning up after animals, you may be happy to learn that tarantula tanks only need to be cleaned out about once a year.

MORE KNOWLEDGE TO SINK YOUR FANGS INTO

A TARANTULA MOLT

While this may sound like an ice-cream soda you'd LOVE to serve to a particularly annoying (perhaps teenage) sibling, it is actually OLD SKIN. As the tarantula grows, she sheds her exoskeleton and produces a new one. This is called "molting." It can take hours to crawl out of the old skin (which is COOL to watch), and

then it can take a few days for the new exoskeleton to harden. Your tarantula may not eat for weeks when going through a molt. This is a very stressful time for spidey, and NOT a good time to consider handling her.

BAD HAIR DAYS, AND OTHER HAZARDS

Tarantulas have special "urticating" (translation: itch-causing) hairs on their abdomens. When they are upset —say, they feel they have not been "treated with respect" — they rub these hairs off and throw them at the person or thing that has disrespected them. The hairs have microscopic barbs, and they can work their way into skin. If they get in a person's eyes, it can be a REALLY bad thing that requires a doctor.

Another potentially painful situation involves the "not very toxic" venom. The Chilean rose and Mexican red-knee tarantulas are really calm, and don't often bite. However, that means

Q: My mother says spiders are repulsive cannibals. Is that true?
A: Yes. It's part of their charm.

Q: Can I keep more than one tarantula in the same tank?
A: Which part of the "cannibal" concept doesn't make sense to you?

Q: I keep hearing people say that tarantulas are really smart. Is this true?
A: Compared to other arthropods, tarantulas have really big brains. Some people think this means they're smart. But it seems to me that being a stand-out in a crowd of arthropods—flies, centipedes, cockroaches—doesn't exactly equate to SMART. I wouldn't expect any help with your homework.

SPEAKING SPIDEY

Here is some tarantula body language, and how to interpret it:

On back, legs in the air = Getting ready to molt

Front legs raised in the air = Do NOT dis me!

Rubbing abdomen with back leg = Preparing to hurl hair at you

Legs underneath body = Sick; or—if accompanied by no movements—dead

they do SOMETIMES bite, and it feels like a bee sting. As with bee venom, some people are allergic to tarantula venom, and for them a bite can be really dangerous.

Those are the major hazards tarantulas pose to humans, but there is ONE big hazard that humans pose to tarantulas. And that has to do with DROPPING them—which is actually pretty common, since people get scared when holding them. Also, tarantulas can easily dart off a person's hand. These spiders have really heavy bodies, so when they fall from even a few feet up, they tend to, uh, go SPLAT. Which is sad and gross. (AND weird, since tarantulas have blue blood.)

SO...TO HOLD OR NOT TO HOLD?

THAT is the question. Carrying a tarantula around is OBVIOUSLY a BODACIOUS thing to do, but there are CLEARLY risks involved. So, this is a decision you have to make WITH your parentals. If you really want a tarantula and you don't like living on the edge, then it's totally cool to have one that's just for WATCHING. You don't have to worry about getting poisonous bites, or being hit by flying hairs, or getting an unexpected view of your tarantula's guts. You can just throw a cricket in there each week, spray water in there, get help cleaning the tank once a year, and you're GOOD TO GO.

TARANTULA TRIVIA...

Male tarantulas make horrible pets. They have one thing in mind: finding girl tarantulas. They forget to eat, they don't like people (unless the people happen to resemble attractive female tarantulas), and they don't usually live longer than a few months, or maybe a couple of years.

Females are calmer and can live for up to 30 years.

Like cats, tarantulas have retractable claws.

When a tarantula gets old, it goes bald.

A tarantula can lose a leg, and it will grow back. (Unless it happens to be an adult male tarantula. They can't seem to get that going, either.)

The Italian town of Taranto had a problem in the 1500s with hairy spiders they thought to have a deadly bite. The people were convinced that the only cure for one of these bites was to dance an extremely energetic dance for hours, or even days, without stopping. Musicians would roam the streets and fields, looking to play music for those afflicted. The dance became known as the tarantella, and the spider: the tarantula.

MONARCH BUTTERFLY

TO imagine this insect in your life, you first have to adjust your thinking on bugs. Monarchs don't eat dirt or suck the guts out of fellow insects. They neither bite nor slime when in a bad mood. In fact, monarchs don't HAVE a bad mood. They are, simply, garden fairies who sip sweet nectar. Monarch butterflies are the gentle poets of the extreme pet world.

But don't get too attached! These are fair-weather friends—you can only have them in the summer.

TWO PETS FOR THE PRICE OF ONE!

Most people who keep monarchs get them when they are babies. And when monarchs are babies, they are a WHOLE different pet — they are CATERPILLARS! These caterpillars are really cool-looking, too – yellow, black, and white striped, with black feelers on their heads and rears. They grow to be around two inches (5 cm) long, and you can hold them (GENTLY!) once they are about half that size. They spend most of their time crawling around on leaves, which—conveniently—happen to be what they eat. But there is only ONE type of plant that has the leaves theylike. Yes, as with most babies, monarchs need their…

Report Card

Coolness	A
Aroma	A
Neatness	B
Ease of Care	B-
Cost Factor	B-

SCI-NAME: *Danaus plexippus*

SIZE: 3 ½-5 in. (9-13 cm) wing span; about 1/50th of an ounce in weight (about as heavy as a small paper clip)

LIFESPAN: Caterpillar: about 2 weeks; Butterfly(non-migrating): 2 to 5 weeks; (migrating): 7 to 9 months

MILK (WEED)

Milkweed plants used to grow wild all over the place, which was GREAT for monarchs. Butterflies afloat on the breeze would spot these fields everywhere, and glide down to lay eggs on the leaves. Caterpillars by the zillion would emerge from the teeny eggs to find an all-you-can-eat buffet right under their sixteen teeny feet. But, alas, milkweed has many enemies in the world. Great fields are cleared for buildings and roads, and weed-despising humans regularly dowse it with chemicals. SO, monarchs have a hard time finding milkweed these days, which means YOU probably will, too. If you don't already have a source, here a few suggestions for finding some:

Go to a nature center and ask a naturalist where to find milkweed. ALL naturalists LOVE milkweed!

Find out what milkweed looks like (the Internet has good pix), and go on an exploration to find it in your neighborhood. Check out overgrown areas by roadsides. If it is summer, find a monarch and follow it!

Grow your own. If you plant seeds, it will be a year before you have enough to raise a few caterpillars, though. You can speed this up by getting milkweed plants at garden centers that specialize in butterfly and habitat gardening. Once you've got an established patch, it will get bigger every year, and you will be able to raise more and more monarchs!

THE ZEN OF CATERPILLAR MAINTENANCE

As soon as milkweed is growing where you live (late spring or early summer), you can get your caterpillars! They will come in the mail with a very important and easy-to-read instruction booklet. Since these wiggly things are SO LITTLE at first, and have a habit of flying off into oblivion on (virtually) invisible strands of silk, GET HELP transferring them into their home habitat.

A 5- or 10-gallon aquarium tank with a lift-off screen top works best for caterpillar living and viewing, but plastic critter containers are also fine. Add some branches for crawling to make things more fun for everyone.

Basically, every day you will be giving them fresh leaves, and you will clean out the old leaves and all the caterpillar poop (of which there will be plenty). This is tricky while they are still little—you need to make sure they are not stuck to the leaves you chuck out!

The caterpillars go through several stages of growth called INSTARS, and they shed after each growth spurt. By the time your monarch caterpillar is full-grown—in approximately two weeks—it will have eaten 20 to 30 milkweed leaves, and shed four times. And THEN, folks, it's…

CHRYSALIS TIME!

When they are plump and ready, your caterpillars will go searching for places to, uh, hang out. Usually this will be the top of the tank, or a branch. Each caterpillar will squeeze some silk and goo from its squirt-gun-like spinneret (which is located in its back end) and hook its rear legs

ASK THE PET WHIZ

Q: I've seen these monarch caterpillars in a field near my house. Can I just get one there and keep it?

A: If it's not someone's private property, and if you don't have some kind of local law against collecting bugs, then SURE! Those must be milkweed plants in that field, too, so you have food for them! Check out the Monarchwatch website for good instructions on how to care for the caterpillars and butterflies.

Q: My monarch butterfly is three days old, and it hasn't eaten yet. Help!

A: That's not a question, but I'll help you anyway. Since they are naturally programmed to go to flowers, you sometimes have to teach them how to drink from a sponge. Pick your butterfly up and gently set it on the nectar-soaked sponge. Do this a couple of times, and it should taste the sweet stuff with its feet, and that will make the proboscis (a long tongue) roll out. If not, you can get a pin and actually roll it out yourself, and guide it into the nectar. You will need some help from parentals for that little operation.

into that, and then drop itself into an upside-down position. Its head will come up a bit, and it will stay in this "J" shape for a few hours. Then some wiggling will begin and—quite suddenly, so don't blink—the skin will shed for the last time, revealing a bright green, blobbish, alien-looking THING. Very soon, though, this will change into a smooth, jade-green chrysalis (a.k.a. pupa) with gold dots that sparkle in the light. And it will stay this way, perfectly still, for about two weeks. Inside, the caterpillar's

Continued on page 113

body is reorganizing into something else. And you will have time to work on…

CREATING YOUR MONARCHY

A monarch's home is his – tent, actually. There are several kinds you can buy, or (FUN DIY PROJECT!) you can make one. Basically the thing has to be made of very fine netting. Once you've got that figured out, put it in a warm, sunny place in your home.

While you are waiting for the butterflies to emerge, you also need to plan for feeding them. A butterfly eats by way of a long tongue called a PROBOSCIS, which stays coiled up under the butterfly's head until it unfurls it to suck nectar out of a flower. SO, you have to mimic this flower situation in your tent, and the easiest way is to put a brightly-colored, clean sponge in a shallow

dish, and keep it wet with nectar. You can purchase a special kind of nectar which never turns sour, or you can plan on making fresh nectar daily in your kitchen. (RECIPE: 1 part sugar to 9 parts water.)

Once you have all this set, you will be ready for your butterfly's…

COMING-OUT PARTY!

On the day of your monarch butterfly's emergence, the chrysalis—after being green for so many days—will become transparent. You will see black, mostly, and some orange. At some point—and it comes with no warning, so you need to watch closely—the chrysalis case will crack open, and the butterfly will pop out and hang upside-down from it. It will look very un-butterfly-like at this point, with a fat body and small, squished-up wings. But keep watching, and you'll see it pump fluid out of its body and into its wings, and in MINUTES it will have a slim, fuzzy,

white-dotted body and big, flat, orange and black wings. The butterfly still needs to hang there, undisturbed, for a couple of hours or so, until the wings dry completely. When the wings begin to flap slowly, then gently slide your finger under the monarch's feet, and it will cling to you while you carefully transfer it into the tent.

CAN YOU HANDLE IT?

Butterflies belong to a scientific order called *Lepidoptera*, which means "scale-wing." If you look at your monarch's wings with a magnifying glass, you will know why! The wings have thousands of tiny, flat scales that overlap like shingles on a roof. This gives the wings their colors, and makes them strong for flight. And, unlike the wings of many butterflies and moths, monarch wings are sturdy enough to touch.

To take a monarch from the tent, find one that has its wings closed. Pick it up with your thumb and index finger by putting them together over the spot where all four wing-parts meet. Then you can lift the butterfly out slowly, and get

Q: What if school is really boring next fall? Do you know how to make a classroom more interesting?
A: Loading your pockets with hissing cockroaches DEFINITELY works. But if you want an idea that won't land you in the principal's office (which is WAY more boring than a classroom), I would suggest MONARCHS! Raise them in midsummer, so you still have them when school starts. Teachers are MAD about butterflies, so you'll probably even be asked to keep them in the classroom. AND, if you show your classmates how to tag and release, you are sure to be GOLDEN with your teacher for the entire year.

a look at it up-close and personal! You'll see the coiled-up proboscis, the compound eyes, the long antennae and jointed legs. TIP: Get help with this until you have the hang of it.

LETTING GO...

Though monarchs live fine in a tent, eating the nectar you make, they are happiest when free. The best thing to do is to keep them for a week or two, and then release them into a garden. Pick a warm, sunny day, and make it a special event—invite your friends and take pictures! When you're ready, put your beautiful bug on your outstretched palm, and watch it take wing.

If you keep your monarch longer than two weeks, it may die. This is just because some monarchs have short lifespans of just two to five weeks. Generally, monarchs born in early or midsummer have these short lives. They fly, drink nectar, mate, and the females lay eggs on the underside of milkweed leaves. Those eggs become the next generation of that family.

Over the course of one summer, there can be many generations of monarch families. They all are pretty much the same until the last generation that emerges in late summer or early fall. These monarchs may sense the shortening days, or the changes in temperature, but entomologists (bug scientists) are not sure what makes them different. They don't look for mates or lay eggs. They head way up into the sky—as high as 10,000 feet (3,048 m) up—and join other monarchs in the annual...

MONARCH MIGRATION!

Like birds and whales, monarchs migrate, or go south to get away from the cold. They travel as far as 3,000 miles (4,800 km) from their summer homes, each day flying about 100 miles (161 km). In six weeks they reach their destination, and rest there for the winter. In March, they turn around and journey north, back to their summer homes. Migrating monarchs can live for eight or nine months.

Most of the monarchs from North America fly to high mountains in Mexico—the same places every year. By the time they get there, so many have joined together that they form massive butterfly clouds that swoop into the forests. In clusters, they land on the trees, covering them so completely that wings are all you can see. The local people call them "mariposa monarca" (monarch butterfly, in Spanish) and take tourists up the mountains to see them.

PLAYING TAG WITH THE MONARCHS

The reason people know where the monarchs go when they migrate is because of something called "tagging." It works like this:

Let's say you live in Cape May, New Jersey, where lots of migrating monarchs stop to eat. You catch a monarch in your big butterfly net, and you put a sticker (tag) on its wing, and then let it go. The sticker has a web address and a number on it, and you add that number, and the date and location, to a tracking list at a website. Then, some months later, the monarch is found in El Rosario, Mexico, where lots of monarchs spend the winter. The person who finds it goes to the website and enters the number, along with the new date and location. Now, when you go back to check the list, you see that your monarch flew all the way to Mexico.

In this same way, YOU can tag YOUR monarchs, too! Order a tagging kit, and the instructions are easy to follow. You may find that your monarchs are world travelers!

MONARCH TRIVIA...

Butterflies taste with their feet! They land on flowers, and their feet tell them if it's worth it to roll out their tongues to eat. They also smell with their antennae.

You can tell a male monarch butterfly because it has black spots (scent scales) in the middle of its hindwings. But it's impossible to tell if a caterpillar is male or female by looking.

Caterpillars have over 1,000 muscles that help them move.

The compound eyes of monarch butterflies are highly developed. They can see more colors of the rainbow than any other animal. They can even see ultraviolet light, which humans can't.

Monarch butterflies can flap their wings 5-12 times per second. (Which is not all that fast, as butterflies go.)

Monarch butterflies are poisonous to birds and other animals that eat them because of toxins in the milkweed they eat when they are caterpillars. An animal that eats a monarch feels horrible and then pukes. They leave all monarchs alone after that.

Butterflies are cold-blooded and need the warmth of the Sun in order to fly.

If you ate and grew at the same rate as a monarch caterpillar, you would weigh as much as a school bus 15 days after you were born.

SILKWORM CATERPILLAR

IN monarch families, it's the ADULT bug that gets all the attention. The BUTTERFLIES are SO beautiful, and get to drink NECTAR all day, and go on TRIPS every year. No one seems to care about the YOUNG monarchs—the poor, lowly caterpillars.

But, thankfully, things are MUCH different in *Bombyx mori* households. KIDS RULE, and grown-ups—small, insignificant moths—are flightless creatures with NO LIFE (well, they live for three days, maybe). Bombyx adults don't even have (IMAGINE A WORLD LIKE THIS) mouths, and their only purpose in life is: the creation of SILKWORM CATERPILLARS.

Yes, THESE caterpillars are appreciated, and HAVE been for thousands of years. At one time, they were part of a worshipped secret in China, and the emperors would have you put to death if you even talked about silkworms. With that in mind, it's probably a good assumption that kids didn't keep them as pets in those days. Today, though, you are free to have ALL the silkworms you want, and even blab away about them!

You may be wondering a few things at this point. Like…

WHAT WAS THE BIG SILKWORM SECRET THAT THE ANCIENTS WERE SO UPTIGHT ABOUT?

WHY DON'T SILKWORM MOTHS FLY?

DON'T ALL GROWN-UPS HAVE NO LIFE?

AND WHAT, EXACTLY, DO YOU DO WITH A PET SILKWORM?

Sit back, my friend, and all will soon be unraveled.

SCI-NAME:	***Bombyx mori***
SIZE:	Caterpillar: 2-3 in. (5-8 cm); Moth: 2 in. (5 cm) wingspan
LIFESPAN:	Caterpillar: 3 weeks; Moth: 1 to 3 days

THE SECRET (OR SECRETION) OF SILK

Legend has it that in 2500 B.C., there was a Chinese empress who—probably bored out of her mind—found herself inspecting a mulberry tree. There, amidst the branches, she saw something that interested her: a blob. (Oh yeah, she was bored.) This was actually a cocoon, which she pulled from the branch. Plucking at it, she discovered it to be made of one very long strand, and she soon found herself with a handful of soft, luminous thread. (And, of course, she would also have found in her hand a now-naked, partially developed moth, which she would probably have smashed under her slipper. But that part was left out of the legend.)

The empress got an idea! She would collect more and more of these blobs, and get more and more thread, and she would make a beautiful robe for her CRUSH, the emperor. Several thousand cocoons later—and after inventing the loom—the empress finally finished the robe. The emperor was so impressed with its majesty and beauty that he declared that no one should know the source of this fine material. China, he said, would be the only producers of the amazing fabric, and China, he said, would become a wealthy dynasty by selling silk to the rest of the world!

And THAT, according to the legend, is why silk was a secret.

There is an alternate ending to the legend, though. ANOTHER theory of why the emperor didn't want the rest of the world to know how the silk fabric was made. It goes like this:

When the delighted emperor asked his wife how she had made this marvelous cloth that would turn China into the envy of the world, she took him to a little workshop she had set up among the mulberry trees. In the shop were many Chinese maidens, some busily unraveling cocoons, some weaving fabric from the thread. The empress then led him to a room from which a strange chomping sound emanated, and there he saw baskets filled with hundreds of caterpillars noisily chewing away on leaves. Other caterpillars, now fat, were spinning cocoons. THIS was the real source of the silk, the empress told her husband, excitedly. It came from silkworm secretions, she said, which turned to soft thread after being spit from glands in their

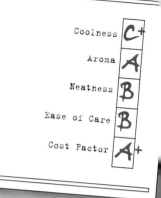

Report Card

Coolness	C+
Aroma	A
Neatness	B
Ease of Care	B
Cost Factor	A+

mouths. Squirming ever so slightly inside his new robe, the emperor began to wonder if the silk trade might have a better chance of success if the customers didn't realize they would be wearing clothes made of insect saliva. The rest, as they say, is history.

THE STRANGE LIFE OF A SILKWORM (AND YOUR STRANGE ROLE IN IT)

Because silkworms were forced into labor so long ago, they have evolved to adapt to the factory life. This is why silkworm moths have useless wings and no mouths. They emerge from their cocoons with many other moths by their sides, so they no longer have a need for wings to fly around and look for mates. Since they don't have to expend that energy, they also don't need to eat.

All you need to be a silkworm caretaker is a cardboard shoebox and mulberry leaves. Mulberry grows late spring through fall in most areas, and is all over the place. Ask a parent or a naturalist to find some trees for collecting leaves.

When you order silkworms, you will get tiny caterpillars that are only days old. Follow instructions that come with them, and transfer them to fresh leaves right away. They won't eat much at first, but as they grow their appetites improve. HUGELY.

For three weeks or more, these caterpillars will eat and grow. You need to provide fresh leaves two or three times a day. They will depend on you! They have no instincts to go looking for leaves. (Which means you can leave the top off if you want, but the leaves stay fresher if the box is closed.) When they are big enough, you will be able to hear them eat, and it's really cool to put the box near your bed and fall asleep to the sound.

When the caterpillars are full-grown (2 to 3 inches, or 5 to 8 cm, long), they will stop eating and turn kind of yellowish. For about three days, they will spin cocoons, and then they will stay in there for about three weeks.

When a moth is ready, it makes a hole in the cocoon and crawls out. Small moths are male, and large ones are female. Within minutes, they mate. By the next day or so, the females should lay eggs—200 to 500 each! These will be stuck to the sides of the box and will be yellow at first. The moths will die very soon after that.

Eggs that turn black are fertilized. Sometimes they will hatch on their own (in about two weeks), but usually they need to be subjected to "winter" in your refrigerator. Put black eggs in a zip-lock bag and chill them for at least a few weeks. Once you take them out, it will be about 6 to 20 days before they hatch. You can actually leave eggs in the refrigerator for up to five years!

Remember, you can only raise
silkworms as long as the mulberry
lasts!

ARTSY WAYS TO HAVE FUN
WITH YOUR PET!

Put your worms to work! Since
silkworms are used to working, you can
get them to make pretty things for you!
Cut out a circle (about four inches, or
10 cm, in diameter) from cardboard,
and tape it to the top of a bottle,
so the neck of the bottle is under
the middle of the circle, and the
cardboard piece is sitting very
flat. When your silkworms
are getting ready to spin,
place one on the cardboard
circle. It will spin its silk
flat, instead of in a cocoon
shape. This will take a
few days, and then you
can put the caterpillar
(who is now a pupa)
back in the box. Peel
the silk gently off
the cardboard.
You can use it as
a bookmark or a
decoration, or
incorporate

it into a collage! If you want to make a thicker one, don't peel it off the cardboard after the caterpillar is done—put a second caterpillar on to give it another layer. You can try different shapes, too, but silkworms seem to have a problem with points and fall off a lot.

HARVEST RAW SILK!

You can collect your own raw silk strands to use for sewing, embroidery, or other creative things. After your moths have emerged, gather up all the cocoons. Get an adult help to boil water in a small pan. Remove the pan from heat, and let it cool for three minutes. Drop one cocoon in the water and let it soak for one minute. Scoop it out with a spoon and place it on a paper towel. When it's cool enough to handle, pick it up and begin to gather thread between your thumb and index finger. It takes a while to get the hang of this, but sort of slowly wiggle the thread away from the cocoon. As it gets longer, wrap it around an empty thread spool. You will get a lot of different strands from one cocoon, and you can twist some together in your palms to make thicker thread, if you want. Repeat the process with each cocoon. (In factories, they boil the cocoon before the moth comes out, so the cocoon doesn't have a hole in it. That way, they can gather the silk in one continuous strand, which is about a mile long!)

BBFY SURVEY

Best Bug For You

So you want one of these skulking X-pets, but you can't decide which is best for you, huh? Well, here's a little survey guaranteed to help you choose that perfect buggy, chum pal! It's psychologically valid, highly scientific, AND fun!

Okay, maybe it's not guaranteed.

And it's not REALLY psychologically valid.

Or highly scientific, for that matter.

To be honest, it probably won't be ANY help at all.

But, HEY, it's FUN! (And isn't that what this is all about?)

For EXTRA AMUSEMENT, take this survey again, but in place of the word "pet" in the line, "HOW IMPORTANT IS IT TO ME TO HAVE A PET THAT..." substitute the word "friend," "girlfriend," or "boyfriend." If you want, think of other words to substitute in. Be creative!

WITH 1 BEING TOTALLY NOT IMPORTANT, AND 5 BEING MONDO IMPORTANT, RATE THE FOLLOWING:

HOW IMPORTANT IS IT TO ME TO HAVE A PET THAT...

— can live without a head for some period of time?

— has hairy legs?

— can scare away stalkers?

— lives longer than a few weeks?

— is generally ugly and repulsive?

— eats dirt, rotten food or other gross things?

— guarantees me plenty of space on the couch when I bring it to family TV night?

— releases toxic bodily fluids when angry?

— pulls out its own hair and throws wads of it at me when I dis it?

SCORING

Add up all your points. If you score between 10 and 25, you are probably a deep enough person to raise monarchs or silkworms. If you score over 25, then cockroaches, millipedes, and the tarantula are probably more your speed. For help narrowing the field to one bug, turn to the next page.

Okay, extreme bug fanatic, you've taken the BBFY Survey, and you've got it down to approximately two favorite bugs. OR—if you have taken the survey and (understandably) rejected the results—you have picked the two bugs you think are the coolest. Enter these pets at the tops of the two columns below and, based on what you have read, list the PROS and CONS.

(TIP: A PRO is something GOOD about the pet, such as the fact that it only needs its tank cleaned once a year; while a CON is something BAD, such as the possibility that it might make you itchy by flinging barbed hairs at you.) Generally, the best pet to get is the one that has the most PROS or the fewest CONS.

COOLEST BUGS

PROS | CONS

PROS | CONS

CHINESE FIRE-BELLIED TOAD

WHEN you think of a toad, do you picture a fat, wart-encrusted lump closely resembling a dirt clod? If so, then YOU haven't met THIS toad. THIS toad is the HOTTIE of toad social circles. Under a cool cape of lime green, it boasts a blazing orange-to-red belly. The glossy tips of its toes are the same flaming shade. And its hypnotic eyes—which bulge from the top of its head—have pupils shaped like HEARTS. The fire-bellied toad is no clod. It is the CUPID of the amphibian world.

WILD FIRE-BELLIES

These little toads are from Siberia, China, and Korea, where they spend most of their time submerged in ponds or

streams. The green color of their backs blends in with floating plants, and with mosses when on land. They are also protected from predators by the mucus on their skin, which has a disgusting taste and irritating effect on animals that attempt to eat them.

THE TOAD ABODE

This toad needs water to swim in, plants to hide among, and a dry area for feeding and basking. There are plastic habitats you can buy that provide wet and dry spots and are designed for easy, daily water changes. There should always be a few inches of water, and it is easiest to use bottled spring water. You can use dechlorinating drops in tap water and let it sit for 24 hours, if you want. Keeping the water fresh and clean is the most important thing!

FIRE-BELLY FEEDING

This toad will go after anything that moves! Crickets work just fine, fed two or three times a week. You can also keep a few guppies in the water, if you want, and your toad may eat one every now and then.

ORIGINAL VALENTINE'S DAY IDEA:

Give your crush a fire-bellied toad! (You may want to include a little warning about its toxic slime coating, but WHATEVER.)

Rep

Coolness	B+
Aroma	A
Neatness	B
Ease of Care	B-
Cost Factor	A-

HOLD IT, TOADY!

You can handle this toad, but it's better not to do it real often. Since they are pretty good jumpers, you have to be careful not to hold them in places where they can get lost or hurt if they leap out of your hands. After touching these toads, you HAVE to wash your hands REALLY well because the toxins can sting or cause allergic reactions, especially if it gets in your eyes or in any cuts.

WATCHING THE TOAD!

These are active little guys, so you may be completely entertained by viewing yours, and not even feel the need to pick him up.

Even watching him EAT can be fun! These toads don't have extendable tongues like many toads do, and they pounce and grab at their prey. SO, don't just dump the crickets in and leave! Grab a box of cereal and veg in front of the tank for a while.

If you keep guppies in the water, the entertainment will be EVEN better. Your toad will NEVER tire of chasing the little fish, and watching this can be a continual source of amusement for YOU.

There's drama, too! When your fire-bellied toad is frightened, she will display her belly, signaling that she is POISON! If on land, she will do something called the "unkenreflex," which means she will lift her front and back legs over her back and arch her belly up.

AND, of course, there HAS to be some HORROR! Shedding time is when you MAY want to put the munchies away. Your toad will bloat up and begin to cough and spit. After a bit a writhing, he will rip the skin off his back, and (ew) start EATING it.

EVERYTHING YOU ALWAYS WANTED TO KNOW ABOUT TOADS, BUT WERE AFRAID TO ASK...

Lots of people wonder about the difference between toads and frogs. The truth is, there really ISN'T a difference. Technically, toads are a type of frog. Many toads have short legs, dry skin, and live on land, so they are easy to identify. But not ALL toads! The fire-bellied toad, for instance, hangs out in the water, has longer legs, and is slime-coated. So, GO FIGURE.

Toads are amphibians. They are cold-blooded and go through a complete metamorphosis, which you probably learned all about in second grade. Adult toads lay eggs in the water, which hatch into tadpoles, which develop into toads, which lay eggs in the water, which hatch into tadpoles. It's like the song that never ends.

Toads absorb water through their skin. This means that when they are thirsty, they just plop down in a

ASK THE PET WHIZ

Q: I have an aquarium with some other critters in it. Can I keep a fire-bellied toad in there with them?
A: Well, first of all, you would have to have a "land" area for the toad, which most aquariums don't have. Second of all, the toad would probably eat some of your "other critters." And, third of all, the rest of your "other critters" would probably be poisoned by the toad toxins (including its pee, which is more toxic than its slime). So, the answer is: not likely.

Q: I want to have a few of these toads. Is that cool?
A: They can live together just fine, BUT you have to have a big, fancy tank with a water pump and filter, and places for the toads to come out. Make sure you do a lot of research and that you can get all the stuff they need. It IS cool to have more than one!

Q: If a frog or toad can make a call that's SO loud it can be heard from, like, MILES away, then how come it doesn't go deaf?
A: You win BEST QUESTION of the day! There IS a reason for this, but it's not well understood. The frog's ears are attached somehow to

Continued on page 131

puddle or take a swim. The oxygen in the water is used by their bodies, too.

Medical researchers are doing experiments to see if frog and toad skin toxins can be used to help relieve pain and fight cancer, which would be totally great!

Herpetologists are scientists who study amphibians and reptiles. The word comes from the Greek "herpeton," which basically means things that crawl around on their bellies. A person who keeps amphibians or reptiles as pets is called a herpetoculturist.

Toads and frogs have REALLY cool EYES. Some have round pupils, some have vertical slits of pupils (which are good for night vision), some have horizontal pupils (good for day vision). And OTHERS have designer eyes, with pupils that are triangular, star-shaped, or—like the fire-bellied toad's—heart-shaped. Amphibians can't see colors—only black and white.

The bones of some frogs and toads form a new ring each year, so scientists who find frog bones can tell how old the critters were.

Toads and frogs have CALLS, which are usually to attract mates, but can also be to claim territory, announce a coming storm, or express pain or fear. In some species, only the males can make noise. Large frogs and toads tend to have deep voices, or low-frequency calls. Small frogs and toads have high chirps, or high-frequency calls. Some calls can be heard from miles away! The male fire-bellied toad has a call that sounds like a small dog barking from a distance away.

A fear of toads is called BUFONOPHOBIA.

ASK THE PET WHIZ

its lungs, and when he makes a call, the ears and lungs vibrate together. Somehow this keeps the thin membrane of the eardrum from breaking, it is thought.

Q: How does a toad feel when he has a broken leg?
A: I know this one! UNHOPPY!

Q: Okay, then. Why did the toad go to the hospital?
A: For a HOPPERATION!

Q: What happened to the frog when his parking meter expired?
A: IT GOT TOAD!

Q: You're GOOD.
A: I know. I'm the WHIZ.

RED-EYED TREE FROG

HAVE you ever seen one of those "Save the Rainforest" posters? You know, the one that has the green frog on it, with blue-and-yellow racing stripes, orange toepads, and ENORMOUS red eyes? Well, guess what? THAT is the red-eyed tree frog, and—OH YEAH—it can be YOURS!

There ARE challenges, though. You have to get a few of these little frogs if you want them to be happy (and hoppy!), so things can get a little expensive. And since these frogs are tropical, it can be hard to get the habitat just right. They also have delicate skin, so you can't handle them a whole lot. But if you're a frog freak and a rainforest fanatic, THIS is a CHOICE X-PET for you!

ESCAPE BY...COLOR?

Since these frogs are so fast and limber, they are EXCELLENT at escaping from their nighttime predators. The daytime, however, presents problems while the frog is trying to catch some Z's. SO...to camouflage itself, it turns into a green lump that blends in with the leaf it chooses for a bed. Its eyes close, all colorful parts tuck tightly under its body. And it stays VERY still. But if it hears or feels something threatening, the frog's eyes BOING open! The bright red circles throw off the hovering animal, and in that split second the frog leaps, flashing blue-and-yellow stripes that give the predator another visual shock. And, hopefully, that is JUST enough time for the frog to make its getaway. This type of defense mechanism is called STARTLE COLORATION.

Report Card

The
Red Eye
Report

Coolness   A
Aroma   A
Neatness   A
Ease of Care   B-
Cost Factor   C-

SCI-NAME: *Agalychnis callidryas*

SIZE: Male 2 in. (5 cm), female 3 in. (8 cm) long

LIFESPAN: 3 to 5 years in captivity

TREE FROGS GOING OUT... OF THEIR MINDS!

In the rainforest home of the red-eyed tree frog, the air is filled with the chattering of monkeys, the squawking of birds and the slithering of snakes. For about half of every year the male red-eyed tree frogs add their chirps to the hum of the forest, too, when they come together in great, orderly groups to stand tall and puff out their throat sacs. Louder and louder they get, quivering and shaking to the music, until—for reasons probably only understood by male tree frogs and rock concert crowds—they suddenly break into a wrestling match. With the beat of the rainforest behind them, they pin the other males down and toss their rivals over the sides of the leaves. This

> **WARNING:**
> The following methods of attraction don't work for humans. In fact, they don't work so great for frogs, either.

goes on until a female happens by, at which point the males calm down, organize themselves again, and jump on her back. The female (probably with an exasperated sigh) continues on her way, occasionally jumping into pools of water to try to unloose the throng of males. One by one they drop off over the course of a few days, and begin, again, their (loony) tunes. The female—apparently in charge of the continuation of the species—finds a leaf overhanging a pond and lays her eggs. When the tadpoles hatch, they slide off the leaf and into the water, where they live the first part of their amphibian lives.

YOUR OWN RAINFOREST ZONE

These string-bean frogs will bring the rainforest alive in your room! Set up a glass tank (20-gallon or 76-liter "tall" aquarium tank with screen top is good for several of these frogs) with lots of big-leafed plants and branches for climbing. Put pesticide-free peat moss and topsoil on the bottom,

Q: I think that "startle coloration" thing is AWESOME! Do you suppose the same sort of thing could work for getting rid of annoying people who won't leave you alone? Like, say, if I dyed my tongue orange with Kool-Aid and stuck it out at the girl who keeps stalking me during lunch, do you think she'd go away?
A: Oh, yeah. SHE'D go away.

Q: Man, it must be COOL to be neon green, electric blue, and rocket red! Don't you think human colors are BORING?
A: DEFINITELY. But you know what's sad? The red-eyed tree frog doesn't KNOW how COOL it looks. Since frogs can't see colors, when this guy catches his reflection in the pond he just sees grays. He must think he's pretty ugly, too, the way other animals dart off when he opens his eyes. SAD.

about two to three inches (5 to 8 cm) deep, and set a big, shallow bowl of water in there. The water should not be deeper than about half the length of your frogs, and it has to be changed every day or two.

To have a rainforest, you need RAIN! So, spray the tank with water a couple of times a day to keep the humidity in the 70%–90% range. (All water used in the tank has to be dechlorinated, so spring water works really well.) The other thing a rainforest needs is WARMTH, so you will probably have to buy an under-tank heater and a light to keep temps in the upper 70sF (25°C) during the day, and lower 70sF (22°C) at night.

Continued on page 137

SEEING RED (OR NOT!)

Because these frogs are nocturnal, they will spend a lot of the daytime plastered to leaves or the sides of the tank, sleeping. And watching them sleep is about as much fun as watching your fridge magnets. SO, in order to increase the excitement, you should get a red light for the tank and turn it on in the evening. Frogs can't see red light, so they think it's completely dark—their favorite time to play! Turn out all the other lights in the room, throw a few crickets in the tank, and watch your frogs bounce around, snatching up bugs with their long, sticky tongues. They'll climb on each other and wacky-wall-walk on the glass with their sucker-pad toes. Leave the red light on all night, and the froggy acrobats will entertain you first thing in the morning, too!

RANDOM RED-EYE TRIVIA

ASK THE PET WHIZ

This frog is also known as the MONKEY FROG, because it is such a great climber!

The rainforests that are home to this frog are threatened by global warming, wetland drainage, pollution, and forest-clearing. Bummer!

Q: SO, how do I get these??
A: Since they are so delicate, mail order is not such a good idea. If you can find a reptile and amphibian show in your area, that is the best place to go. Some pet stores carry these, too, but you have to make sure the frogs are healthy. Go in the evening when they are more apt to be active, and make sure they are leaping around the cage.

To express different moods, these frogs can turn darkish green or reddish brown.

The species name callidryas means "beautiful tree sprite" in Greek.

UGLY FROGS!

ARE you into unsightly pets? Do you enjoy the companionship of the repulsive, misshapen, or gruesome? Well, guess what? It turns out you're not REALLY that weird! Here are some surprisingly popular amphib pets that are OOGLY!

WHITE'S TREE FROG (AKA DUMPY TREE FROG)

Lots of people are grossed out by this frog's skin, which is REALLY rubbery. The color ranges from alien-green to humanoid-beige, and there are fatty bulges that lop over the legs and ears and sometimes completely cover both eyes. The oversized, over-lumpy and over-sticky toepads also contribute to the general horror of this hopper. But as a pet, this tree frog is much sturdier than the red-eyed, so you can hold it a whole lot more (assuming you can stomach that). As big as your palm when full-grown, this frog is arguably the largest tree frog on Earth—and unarguably the STRANGEST. Doubles, also, as a Halloween decoration. Possible names for your White's tree frog: Frankenstein, Marvin the Martian, The Mask, Incredible Hulk, or Prince Charming (but I wouldn't let anyone see you kiss this frog, if I were you).

THE PAC MAN FROG

When you get a young Pac Man frog at the pet store— where they are often sold—it will be SO CUTE! Its small,

Dumpy Tree Frog

round body will be covered with artsy spots, and it will have nifty horns over each eye. And the mouth! You'll think it is SO NEAT the way it's as WIDE as the whole body! And you'll take your new baby home, and settle it into a tank, and in a few months you'll be looking at it in there, and you'll be thinking: AAAHHHH!!!

Because Ms. Pac Man will now be a hideous mass the size of a personal pizza, and she will be living up to her name by consuming everything within reach of her mouth (which will STILL be as wide as her entire body). She will have sunk into one spot in her tank, where she will be sitting all day and all night, waiting there for food to arrive. You will probably have given up handling her, too, since she will have also begun mistaking your FINGERS for food. (OUCH.)

That's not to say this frog is mean—just HUNGRY. If you LIKE pets with a good appetite, then this is certainly one to consider. You can throw in bugs, fish, even MICE, and it will gobble them enthusiastically. (Don't even CONSIDER getting two of these frogs, by the way, because you'll be down to one in a matter of SECONDS.) Even though this frog is one of the largest in the world—up to seven inches (18 cm) in diameter—it doesn't need a big tank, because it doesn't really MOVE. And the BEST thing about this blobbish X-pet (at least if you are a *Star Wars* fan), is that it bears a remarkable resemblance to the supremely ugly and infamous Jabba the Hutt.

THE AMERICAN TOAD

These disgusting, yet endearing, toads are VERY down-to-earth—-literally. They spend all their time on the ground, eating bugs, and they basically look like dirt clods—all lumpy, with bumps and warts everywhere. These toads do not have a coating of slime over their skin, but they do ooze out poisonous goo when they find themselves in the mouth of a predator. When picking up one these, you are not in much danger of getting squirted with this stuff (unless, of course, you decide to pop the thing in your mouth—in which case you deserve it), but you will likely have to deal with the toad's first line of defense: They pee when they want to be put down.

But, HEY, this pet is free! Since American toads (or other very similar species) live wild in much of the country, you may be able to go outside on a summer evening and catch one. Set up a natural terrarium with dirt, dead leaves, plants, and a water dish, and you can replenish it with bugs

American Toad

each day or so. Earthworms are easy to dig up, and it's fun to watch the toad shoot out its long, sticky tongue and slurp it in like a piece of fat spaghetti. When it's swallowing, watch the toad's eyeballs disappear into its head for a second—like all frogs, these toads use their eyes to help push food down their throats. Occasionally, you can feed it a firefly, which can be pretty entertaining. Turn the lights out before you drop a live firefly in the tank, and you should catch a glimpse of the toad's belly lighting up like a lantern! (NOTE: Fireflies can be toxic to some toads, so you can't go crazy with this!) If you live where it gets cold, make sure you let this toad free before winter comes so it can prepare to hibernate in the muck.

Pac Man Frog

TADPOLES

IF you want some of these young slimers, then pull on your hiking boots, slather on the bug repellent, and get ready for some swamp-stomping. Tadpoles aren't just a pet—they're an ADVENTURE!

HOW TO HUNT A TADPOLE

The basic supplies: a bucket and a pond net.

Go to ponds or wetlands where there are no rules against collecting critters. Usually parks have rules, but you can always ask a naturalist for help finding frog hangouts.

Spring is the best time to go on a tadpole hunt, and ESPECIALLY after a rainstorm. You'll get muddy, but you'll also get to see and hear a whole lot of toads and frogs— they LOVE the rain.

For safety, you should always be with someone else when hanging out near the water! Take a friend, if that's okay

Tadpole

Not a Tadpole

with your parents, and stay where the water is shallow. (That's where the tadpoles are, anyway!)

Scoop some water into your bucket, and then walk around the edge of the pond to find a good place to net. If the Sun is shining on the water, you may see some tadpoles swimming around, so you'll know you've found the spot!

Squatting at the water's edge, reach out and dip the net with a quick down-and-up motion TOWARD YOURSELF AND THE SHORE. This helps direct them into the net and not out into deeper water. Depending on how many tads are around—or how long it takes you to get the hang of netting—you may have to scoop a bunch of times before you get any. (And you may need to change places a few times, too. Be patient!)

Each time you get a tadpole into your net, slide it into the bucket. When

you've got four or five, you are GOOD TO GO!

BRINGING YOUR NEW POND PALS HOME

Pour a couple of inches of pond water into a clean glass aquarium tank or plastic critter carrier. (They need to be able to swim freely, but the water shouldn't be too deep.) Put gravel or sand in a pile on one end of the tank to make a little "land" area. Add your tadpoles.

You will need to change the water weekly to keep them healthy. If you live close to the place where you collected the tads, you'll be able to get fresh pond water to do this. If that's too difficult, you can use spring water.

There are a couple of options for feeding. Algae (pronounced AL-jee) is the best food, since that is what they eat in the wild. Algae is green slime that grows naturally in ponds and wetlands, and you can find it clinging to sticks and rocks. You can scrape it off with a spoon, or your fingers (if you like that SLIPPERY feel), and drop a glob of it in the tank every couple of days.

If getting algae is too much of a hassle, you can feed them lettuce or spinach. Take a dark green leaf, and—getting help in the kitchen—boil it in some water till it's kind of goopy. Let it cool, then drop it in the tank.

That's all your wigglers will need to grow and turn into frogs in a few weeks.

Or not.

METAMORPHIC MYSTERIES

Your tadpoles will swim around happily, breathing water through their gills and eating delicious, slimy meals you lovingly prepare for them. Back legs will suddenly burst from their bodies, and then

Report Card

Coolness	C+
Aroma	A
Neatness	B
Ease of Care	A-
Cost Factor	A

ASK THE PET WHIZ

Q: Yesterday I went out netting and got a whole bunch of really little tadpoles AND some other cool-looking things that were swimming around in the water. This morning, I noticed that all my tadpoles were gone. Uh, what happened?

A: This may come as a great surprise to you, but a pond is, basically, a big, underwater restaurant. You probably caught some dragonfly larvae, which are hungry, carnivorous buglets that live in the water. When big enough, they can DEFINITELY eat little tads. I suggest you go out netting again today and leave the "other cool-looking things" behind this time.

Continued on page 145

front legs will shoot out where the gills were, causing your tadpole to joyfully rise to the surface to fill their new lungs with air. Mouths and eyes will then change shape, and tails will get sucked up into their bodies—giving them the nutrition they need while they make their final morph into frogliness. But THIS isn't news to you—you know ALL about amphibian metamorphosis. There IS something, though, that you DON'T know.

The thing about netting for tadpoles is (as Forrest Gump said about a box of chocolates, and life) you never know what you're gonna get. You see, in any given swamp or pond, there can be a half dozen different frogs or toads that lay eggs, which means there can be that many different tadpoles swimming around. AND,

each different type takes a different amount of time to develop—some can take weeks, while others can take a WHOLE lot longer. SO, since it can be a real bummer feeding and watching a tadpole that seems to just stay the same week after week, or even month after month, here is some advice:

Though you may be attracted to the biggest tadpoles out there, they are more likely to be bullfrogs, which can take up to TWO YEARS to turn into frogs. They can be HIGH MAINTENANCE, too, often tiring of eating green slime, and taking bites out of any smaller tadpoles you happen to have. HINT: Leave the biggest tads in the pond.

A tadpole that already has back legs is definitely a good catch (literally!). It should turn into a frog in days, or weeks.

Getting eggs instead of tadpoles can sometimes help you identify the species. If you see a long string of clear slime with black dots running through it, then you have probably found toad eggs. Pull off a small part of the string (each dot will become a tadpole!) and put it in your water. Toads are fun to raise because they develop in a matter of weeks. The toad is only about a half inch (1.3 cm) long when it hops out of the water, but it's really cute!

Go to a nature center and ask the naturalists which toads and frogs live in your area. They can show you pictures (or live specimens, if they have them) of eggs, tadpoles, and the frog to help you identify the type you may want to raise. Once you know the species, you can also do a search for pictures and information on the web or in the library.

Tadpoles develop faster in warm water, so pick a place for the tank that is not cold.

IS THERE LIFE AFTER LEGS?

When your tadpoles turn into frogs or toads, you will probably need to take them back to the pond or wetland, and release them near the water. Most frogs are very hard to keep, especially when young. If they are tiny, they need tiny bugs, and catching little ants or aphids every day can get really tedious. Also, many frogs need lots of water for swimming, and will do much better in the pond they came from.

Q: I've seen "grow-a-frog" kits for sale. Can I get my tadpoles that way?
A: Yes, but there can be some ISSUES. Usually, those tadpoles are not the types that naturally live in your area, so you can't release them once they change to frogs. So you can end up with a bunch of frogs that you have to feed and take care of, and that's not usually really successful. If you have a pond you can net in, then I recommend you do that instead. You'll save some bucks, too, man!

Q: Can I hold my tadpoles?
A: VERY slippery critters, these tadpoles, but YES, you can hold them. They have to stay wet, so if you put a little water in your hand, and then drop a tad in your palm (with, say, a small net), you could keep it there for a little while. Not a true pet-bonding experience, I guess, but it's kind of cool to feel their wiggliness and look at them close-up like that. FACT: Tadpoles can keep on living even if a pond dries out, as long as their skin stays moist.

Continued on page 146

It may be hard to say good-bye to your little buds, but remember that they will be a whole lot happier in the wild! And, it's kind of nice, sometimes, to have a pet that you only need to take care of for a few weeks or months. AND, you can always go back and get some more tadpoles!

Q: You know what? I can see RIGHT through my tadpole's skin. WHAT is that spirally thing??

A: It's the intestine! It's all long and coiled because tadpoles are, basically, vegetarians, and plant food is harder to digest. When your tad turns to a frog or toad, the intestine will straighten out because bugs are easier to digest than algae. But you won't see the intestine then. Hopefully.

DO you sometimes have visions of yourself strolling through the woods with a peculiar one-footed pet, leaving a sparkling trail of ooze behind on the path? (In this vision, the pet is leaving the ooze trail, not you. Right?) Are you known for drawing pictures of animals with eyeballs at the ends of long, bobbing stalks and slime dripping from their pores?

No, no, you haven't gone SCI-FI on us, my extra-ordinary friend. You just OBVIOUSLY crave the companionship of...

SLUGS!

Report Card

Coolness (for lovers of slime)	A
(for the other 6 billion people on the planet)	F
Aroma	B
Neatness	B
Ease of Care	A
Cost Factor	A+

SCI-NAME: *Gastropoda pulmonata*

SIZE: 1½–6 in. (3.8–15 cm)

LIFESPAN: About 2 years

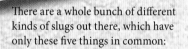

There are a whole bunch of different kinds of slugs out there, which have only these five things in common:

- People despise them to the point of phobic fear.

- The experience of stepping on them barefoot on dark summer nights results in people joining a local chapter of SS (Slug Survivors).

- People make a hobby of plotting strange and unusual methods for their demise, mostly involving salt and beer.

- And when this doesn't work, people visit the anti-slug aisles of their nearest home improvement stores and buy special anti-slug boots and equipment to protect them in their gardens.

- And when THAT doesn't work, they purchase used army tanks on eBay and lie in wait behind a bush in their yards.

Well, actually, that's not the complete truth. The different kinds of slugs out there have WAY more than five things in common. FOR INSTANCE..

- They each have a tongue called a RADULA, which is covered with little teeth that scrape at leaves and mushrooms and other things they eat in the wild.

- They have four tentacles—the bottom two being short sensors, and the top two being long, skinny eyestalks that they can stick way out and wiggle around OR pull completely inside their heads.

They move by creeping along on one big foot. Their muscles ripple in a wave motion, which propels them forward.

They have a big hole (a pneumostome) near the head that opens and closes as they breathe.

AND—last but not least—they ALL are SLIME MACHINES.

THE THINGS YOU NEED TO KNOW ABOUT SLUG SLIME

According to slug scientists, slugs spend about 70% of their energy producing slime. Compare this to human adults, who use about 70% of THEIR energy telling you to

finish your homework. Just kidding! (Everyone knows it's closer to 90%.)

Slugs use slime for movement. They secrete mucus from glands and glide along on this path of smooth, slippery slime. They can climb up walls— even glass—with it.

A slug's slime coating keeps it from drying out and also helps it breathe. This works the same way as the mucus (aka SLIME) that lines our lungs. Slime, as it turns out, is great at helping with gas exchange—which is what breathing is, basically.

Slug slime is also a defense mechanism. When threatened, slugs hump up their bodies and produce a thicker, grainier mucus. Animals that find this in their mouths gag and retch, and then tend to steer clear of slugs for all eternity.

When a slug is REALLY upset it makes SUPER sticky and somewhat bubbly slime.

Slugs can communicate danger to other slugs with their slime. When a slug is out slithering around and it happens upon some grainy, thick, sticky, bubbly slime left by a threatened or upset slug, it knows to make a U-turn and swiftly run away. (Or, more accurately, slowly slide away.)

Slugs sometimes eat each other's slime. (Enough said.)

And just when you thought there could not POSSIBLY be anything ELSE a slug does with its slime…

Slugs use it to get the party started! When a slug wants company, it releases a chemical in its slime. Other slugs in the vicinity smell it and head on over to hang out.

FOR A REALLY GOOD SLIME, KEEP YOUR OWN SLUGS!

Finding slugs is VERY easy, and they are FREE! When the weather is warm, poke around in your yard or in the woods. Look under rocks, logs, or leaves. You will find a sleeping slug clinging there—guaranteed! Another tried-and-true method is to go out at night with a flashlight and look at any paths around your garden. Slugs are nocturnal, so they are SUPER easy to find on a sticky, summer night.

When you find your slug, scoop it up with any leaves it might be on and put it in a critter keeper or glass aquarium tank. (You can keep several slugs together in one tank—they don't fight or anything.) Make sure it has an escape-proof top! Plop more of the earthy stuff into the container—dirt, sticks, rocks, and dead leaves are slug faves. Find a clean spray bottle and fill it with spring water. You have to use this a few times a day to keep the slug's home moist. You don't want it WET, just always moist, so the slug doesn't dry out.

To keep your slug well-fed, you can give it a variety of green leaves from

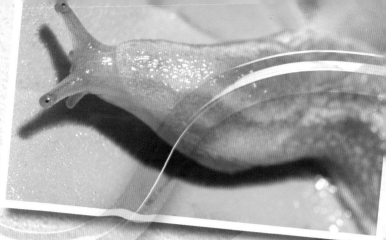

your garden, or just share your own food! Each slug seems to have its own favorite foods, but you might start with cucumber slices, green lettuce, kale, or other healthy stuff. Lots of slugs like sweet things, too, so you can share an occasional (really small, or your slug will die from a sugar surge) piece of cake!

After a while, it's nice to release your slug back where you found it. You can always get more!

AND NOW, A WORD ABOUT YOUR FUTURE... WITH SLUGS!

Q: I read somewhere that people sometimes lick live slugs. Is this true?

A: A long time ago, when (some) people had toothaches they would put slugs in their mouths and let them slither around. The slime was said to have a numbing effect. Thankfully, we have dentists now, so there is no need to do this anymore. Some people do EAT slugs and snails when cooked in a French sort of way—as escargot. Anyone who licks live slugs, though, is probably (how to put this gently...) MENTAL.

An understanding and appreciation of slugs is BOUND to increase your chances of success in life. To start with, you will likely impress your teacher (although it may

Continued on page 152

be best not to actually TAKE any slugs to school until you've scoped out his or her personal feelings on the subject). There are lots of interesting things to discover about slugs and slime, and MANY could become actual careers! To get started, you could…

Do a comparison between the sticky slime of angry slugs and different kinds of glues you buy at the store. This would be a good science fair project, and if you took it a step further, you could probably make your own slug slime glue. You could be the next Elmer!

Test different things (peanut butter, vinegar, soap) to see which is best for removing slime from skin and clothing. You might even find your own special blend of things and start a business selling it! People who work with slugs would welcome a product like this. (Of course, that's a limited market.)

On the flip side, you could create a hand lotion with SLUG SLIME as an ingredient! According to someone named W. T. Fernie (who published findings a hundred years ago, and it's unclear if anyone has furthered the studies since), slug slime can relieve dry, cracked skin. Suggestion: Don't include the words "slug," "slime," or "secretion" in your product name.

Create shimmering artistic designs by letting your slugs glide around on dark-colored sheets of art paper. If you collect enough of these, you can put together an original show for a modern art museum!

ASK THE PET WHIZ

Q: I learned that slugs aren't really male or female. Hm. What does THAT mean?
A: Slugs, my inquisitive friend, are HERMAPHRODITIC. This means a slug can change into a male OR a female—whichever it chooses. This may seem pretty weird, but think how HANDY a power like that could really be! Let's say you have a teacher who gives A's ONLY to GIRLS. Well, then, YOU become a GIRL, and your grades improve instantly! OR (for the girls out there) imagine you are finally at a sleepover with the POPULAR GIRLS, but they IGNORE you ALL NIGHT. You just pop into the bathroom, and—PRESTO-CHANGO— you are a BOY, and all the girls are shrieking and running in circles! (Hehehe.)

Q: How BIG can a slug get?
A: The biggest slug in North America is the *Ariolimax columbianus*, or (in English) the banana slug. And, yes, it looks like a banana, and it can get to be about 8 inches (20 cm) long! The banana slug lives on the West Coast, but there are plenty of big slugs in other parts of the country, so don't worry! The spotted garden slug (*Limax maximus*) is usually around 4–6 inches (10–15 cm) in length, and those are EVERYWHERE.

Pet Whiz Publications brings you…

A MOST EXCELLENT DIY GUIDE ON HOW TO CONVINCE YOUR PARENTS TO GET YOU THE AWESOME PET YOU'VE WANTED YOUR ENTIRE LIFE

(or at least a week).

Top Ten Parent Responses to the Extreme Pet Request

10. Did you hit your head or something?

9. You can't remember to brush your hair, so how are you going to take care of THAT?

8. No, our [cat, dog, baby] will eat it.

7. No, your [dad, teenage sister, cat, dog] is allergic.

6. Dinner is ready. Go wash your hands.

5. No, it bites.

4. No, it stinks.

3. HAHAHAHAHAHAHAHAHAHAHAHAHA

2. Is your homework done?

1. How 'bout a goldfish?

IF you have met with these types of (outrageous!) reactions when asking for your dream pet, then you probably need to work on your approach. To soften up your parents by way of confusion, worry and other exploitative (but absolutely necessary) means, follow this step-by-step plan!

STEP 1

SET THINGS UP BEFORE ASKING YOUR PARENTS

I know this probably seems excessive, but HELP AROUND THE HOUSE. While actually SMILING, do chores BEFORE you are asked. The more boring or gross the task, the better this works. Weed or diaper-related jobs are especially effective for pressuring—er, impressing your parents.

STRUT YOUR A's. Whenever you get a good grade make a HUGE DEAL about it. Hang it on your parents' bathroom mirror, or—even better—on the front door! If they are especially distracted or self-absorbed sorts, tape it to your shirt (or forehead, if necessary) and wear it to dinner!

This may be asking the impossible, but KEEP YOUR ROOM NEAT. Get some large bins that fit under your bed, and scoop everything into them daily. Your parents will be SO happy to see the floor! (No one knows why parents are fixated with seeing the FLOOR, but there you are.)

TIP: Don't toss any food into the bin, unless the pets you want are mice and ants.

Play LET'S MAKE A DEAL! (This only works for the professional underachiever who has convinced his parents he is not intellectually capable of anything above a C.) Say to your parents one day, "If I get all A's this quarter, will you get me a [fill in with pet]?" When they stop laughing, they will say, "Yeah, SURE." At the end of the quarter, while holding up a straight-A report card, you remind them of their promise!

BECOME AN X-PET EXPERT! You'll never connive—er, convince your parents to let you have an extreme pet unless you can counter their arguments against it, and the ONLY way you have ANY chance of doing this is to KNOW it ALL.

This phase can take weeks or even months, depending on how self-disciplined you are. (For some of you, I suppose, it could take years.) You will know you are done when your parents are stopping strangers on the street to tell them what a PERFECT child you are. If you have siblings, this will also be about the time they cease speaking to you altogether.

STEP 2

PICK THE RIGHT SETTING TO BRING UP THE PET TOPIC WITH YOUR PARENTS

Choosing the right time and place to approach your parents and ensnare—I mean SHARE with them is of MAJOR importance... .

The dinner table can be a great spot, on a night when your mother or father has cooked. (If your family is like most, you may have to wait a few weeks before this happens.) Make flattering comments about the cuisine, while shoveling large forkfuls into your mouth. When your cheeks are completely packed with food, ask for the pet. Though they won't understand a word you've said, they will—hopefully—nod and smile in your direction. That's when you swallow and thank them profusely, telling them, first, that they are the best parents on Earth.

Popping the question after an emotionally charged movie can work, too. (*FINDING NEVERLAND* or *FORREST GUMP* are possibilities, or any movie in which a dog dies.) While you are staring at the credits and listening to the sad-ending music, confide in your parents that you have always wanted a: HORSE. They will—patiently, since you are a perfect child and they are in a vulnerable state—tell you that they are so sorry, it is not possible to get one because horses are far too expensive. Sniffling back a few tears, you then ask the REAL question.

If you have a parent who is an obsessive runner, then you are probably familiar with the VERY GOOD mood he or she often is in after a run. (For the unfamiliar...this is caused by endorphins, which are natural chemicals that surge through the bodies of distance runners, briefly making them VERY HAPPY AND MELLOW.) Greet your parent at the door after a particularly vigorous run and immediately ask for the pet. You will, of course, get a huge, sweaty hug as soon as your endorphin-crazed parent sees you there, but who said getting an X-pet wouldn't come with a few risks?

OKAY! Time to brainstorm! What settings might work best for YOU?

OTHER SETTINGS THAT MAY WORK:

When parent is in the shower.

When parent is mowing the lawn.

In the hospital recovering from surgery.

After regaining consciousness following an incident involving an opponent's lacrosse stick, while still flat on back and looking up into parents' worried faces.

How to convince parents:

STEP 3

SETTLE ON THE RIGHT WORDS BEFORE BRINGING THINGS UP WITH YOUR PARENTS

There are many different types of parents out there, and many different ways to ask a question. You need to speak a language your own, personal parent will understand (or NOT!). To help you come up with the best words to trick—I mean, PICK!—check out these sample questions, each matched to parental type.

If your parent is an INTELLEC-TUAL, you might say…
"I am beginning a study of the classification of various arthropods, and it would benefit my research immensely if I could obtain some live specimens, such as the *Archispirostreptus giga* or *Gromphadorhina portentosa*. Okay?"

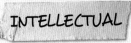
INTELLECTUAL

If your parent is a HEALTH NUT, consider…
"I just saw an article in *Prevention* magazine that says pets can lower your blood pressure, cure depression, AND boost your

HEALTH NUT

immune system! How many should we get?"

If your parent is a NEW-AGER, you may have luck with…
"I think my life would be in complete balance if I had two pets—one named Yin and the other named Yang. Oh, and do you think you could do that feng shui thing so we can find the best place for the cage?"

NEW-AGER

If your parent is a NATURE FREAK, try… (NEVER MIND. If your parent is a nature freak, you probably have extreme pets in your LIVING ROOM.)

NATURE FREAK

If your parent is a SERIOUS sort, you may need to start by saying…
"After this PBS program on Henry the Fourth's library, could I ask you a little question, Mother?"

SERIOUS

OR, if your parent is more on the JUVENILE side, it might be more like... "DAD! Could you turn off 'THE SIMPSONS' for JUST a second?"

If your parent is HYPER AMBITIOUS, you could have luck with... "I went to HYPER AMBITIOUS Yale's website and saw a survey of things all the students had in common, and YOU KNOW WHAT? They ALL had interesting pets when they were kids!!"

PARENTS

TYPE	HOW TO ASK

STEP 4

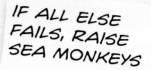

IF ALL ELSE FAILS, RAISE SEA MONKEYS

VENUS FLY-TRAPS

Carnivorous plants are cheap AND mildly entertaining! This one actually eats bugs, and scraps of hamburger meat—what could be better?

CHIA PETS

Okay, this is scraping the barrel as pets go, but it can be a FUN TIME! They come in a variety of animal shapes, including turtles, cows, and frogs. AND you can get celebrity animal Chias, like Scooby-Doo and Shrek's donkey friend!

SEA MONKEYS

If you are (SIGH) unsuccessful at talking your parents into letting you have an extreme pet, DON'T DESPAIR! There is always tomorrow, and WHO KNOWS what kind of mood they will be in. (I mean, we're talking PARENTS here, aren't we?) In the meantime, here are some EXTREME NON-PETS that you may find amusing.

Your parents will perk up when you mention these, because THEY used to order them when THEY were kids, from ads in the back of ARCHIE comic books, or by sending in those little jokes from Bazooka bubble gum. YOU SEE...ordering weird things in this way was a pastime of the boomer generation youth. After buying and chewing hundreds of pieces of bubble gum, they would send away for FREE THINGS, like X-RAY GLASSES! MINIATURE SPY CAMERAS! SEA MONKEYS! And they would RUN to get the mail EVERY DAY to see if their stuff arrived, until FINAL-LY—ten months later—the PRIZE PACKAGE CAME! But (and this may explain why boomer parents tend to be a bit suspicious, and are easily disappointed) the X-Ray Glasses did NOT actually let you see through someone's clothes, as promised, AND there was no way to develop the tiny pictures you took with the Miniature Spy Camera. Sea Monkeys, of course, were also a disappointment, because they didn't look a THING like monkeys. They WERE sort of interesting, though, because they DID seem to be an actual living SOMETHING. Since your parents didn't have the Internet, they probably never could figure out WHAT those things really were. I suggest you take your parent by the hand, search the Internet, and you can learn about these bizarre little critters together. They will surely order a bunch for you, and will be SO excited to find that nowadays there are WAY more fun things to do with them!

AND IF THEY GET EXCITED ENOUGH, MAYBE YOU CAN REVISIT THAT EXTREME PET ISSUE!

INDEX

PHOTO CREDITS